Just Last Year

Karen Mckenna

DEDICATION

To my children

How did I get so lucky?

CHAPTER 1

As the train slowly entered the station and finally stopped, Jen hugged Laura one last time, squeezing her small frame tightly, and kissing the top of her head.

'Are you sure you are going to be okay Mum?' Laura asked, searching Jen's eyes for any sign of weakness.

'Of course I'm going to be okay, don't be silly, you just be sure to look after yourself and please message me as soon as you get back'

'You message me as soon as you get back'

'That will be in five minutes, even I can manage to get home safely from here'

'Are you sure you are okay? I hate leaving you on your own'

'I'm not on my own I have Muffin, anyway you will be back before we know it for your birthday, now quickly get on or you will miss it'

Jen held her breath and fixed her smile. Watching Laura, her little Lolly, struggling to manoeuvre the train doors with her enormous backpack and holdall, she thought she still looked about 12 years old, even with the vibrant violet hair.

You must breathe, just keep breathing. She pressed her fingernails into her palms to stop the tears.

The doors closed, and the train started moving away. Jen searched the windows for a last glimpse. There she was, squeezing herself and her bags onto a seat on the far side. She stayed on the platform, rooted to the spot, the smile still stapled onto her face, but the tears now pricking at her eyes. Breathe, just breathe, her heart now pounding in her chest. One, two, three, four. The platform emptied, but still she stood and watched as the train disappeared around the bend and out of the village.

If she made sure not to move an inch before the train was completely out of sight, everything would be okay, and Lolly would be kept safe.

The grey chill January morning seemed to stand motionless with her, the only movement her shallow breaths and her fists rhythmically twitching as she continued pushing her nails into the fleshy bottom of her palms. One, two, three, four.

She turned and walked quickly up the path away from the station towards the car park, pulling her grey waterproof jacket tightly around herself. In the driver's seat she looked at her reflection in the mirror and saw the panic in her eyes. Then the tears came, warm against her cold face. 'Breathe', she said to the reflection, 'Just sodding well breathe'

She took deep breaths, in through her nose and out through her mouth one, two, three, four and blew her nose. She looked into the mirror again.

'Look at yourself, you are a bloody mess you stupid woman'

She drove out of the empty car park, along almost empty village roads, passing the pub, the infant school, the bakery, hairdressers and newsagents. All was quiet apart from a small group of dog walkers chatting on the village green in front of the church, the three dogs sniffing at each other. The leaden sky threatened rain, the day seemingly unimpressed to leave its night-time mantle.

Jen drove over the stone bridge that crossed the stream and through the iron gates. The gravel driveway swept in a majestic arc leading to the glossy black door of the elegant Georgian building, Millstone House. Driving to the side of the house, along a narrow road, the crunch of gravel under her tyres changed to concrete as it continued behind a tall laurel hedge and a high stone wall. She stopped, parking her small car in front of a red brick and flint cottage.

An estate agent would have called their home 'characterful'. A red brick porch led into a kitchen featuring terracotta floor tiles, hand painted cupboards and a small table and chairs. A door from here led into a cosy beamed sitting room with two sofas, an open fire with a wood burner and a wooden staircase which twisted its way up to two bedrooms and tiny bathroom.

The cottage was an eclectic blend of lovingly refurbished furniture and original pieces of artwork, from the hand painted chests of drawers to the patchwork quilts, everything was touched by Laura's creativity and imagination, Fliss called it shabby chic.

The house still smelled of Christmas, a blend of pine from the now sad little tree in its pot in the corner and cinnamon and clove spices from the burned down candles in the hearth. She will take it all down today, Christmas was over in this house.

Other years they had left everything until the last possible day, the cottage always looking rather bleak at first when the lights and decorations were packed away for another year, magic to mundane.

She went out of the back door and into the little shed opposite to collect the Christmas decoration boxes, there was little storage space in the cottage, so the shed was always full.

Sorting through the various boxes was even more painful than the dying remnants of their family Christmas. Each box held such tender memories, the shoe boxes Laura had decorated at preschool with wrapping paper and red painted pasta shells, the wicker basket that had seen so many picnics in its day and the special little chest with the carved 'L' that had contained Laura's toys when she was little. The anticipated joy of unpacking the boxes three weeks ago, now unimaginable.

'Come on, just get on with it, stop wallowing'
Jen packed everything away as quickly and neatly as she could and returned the boxes carefully to the back of the shed. She then filled the kettle, making tea in her favourite mug and with her mobile phone safely by her side, curled up into a corner of a sofa pulling a fleece throw over herself. Muffin jumped up next to her, curling up as closely as he possibly could, his soft brown eyes saying more than any words of comfort. Jen hugged him closely to her and covered him with the throw.
'I know Muffy you're going to miss her too'
She opened the new book, that Laura had bought her for Christmas, the latest Kathy Athkin. She had been saving it for today, a treat and a distraction. Four chapters in and the sudden chime of a message made her jump. Thank god, all was okay, Laura was back safely. She breathed a sigh of relief and put her book down, realising she did not remember anything she had read in the last two chapters. That was okay, there was plenty of time to read them again. She imagined Laura in her small room, pictures on the walls and strings of pretty lights twisted around the curtain pole and headboard. She would be sitting cross-legged on her bed, earphones in, listening to her music, new furry slipper boots on her feet and a big mug of hot chocolate and marshmallows by her side. Yes, that was a lovely image, if she could just keep that in her head for the rest of the day, she could relax.
Thank goodness, all was well with their world and everything was as it should be. Now she could make some toast and another mug of tea, then take Muffin for a walk and return to re-read those last two chapters. Then another day would be nearly over. You get used to anything eventually, she kept telling herself.
Laura had started her fine arts degree in October. Together they had shared in the excitement of the whole adventure of starting university life. It was certainly not a world Jen knew anything about, but she quickly learned.

Exams, waiting for results, choosing the most suitable courses, filling in endless application forms, visiting hoped for choices, then waiting, the endless waiting.

They had both burst into tears and then laughter when the offer had come through from Laura's first choice. She was incredibly talented and had worked tirelessly, she so deserved to be given this opportunity. Everything was going to plan, although of course the consequences of everything going to plan was the loss of her little girl. It was the price she always knew she would eventually have to pay, but right now she felt she had been robbed. If she could go back would she change anything? How far back?

Once everything had been confirmed, the following months had flown by. Lists of essential items were added to daily, purchased and then crossed off. Books, clothes, kitchen items, bedding, laptop, lists and lists and lists.

When the departure day finally arrived, they had somehow managed to cram everything into Jens small car and with the help of Fliss's sat nav and printed instructions for back up, had made the nearly three hour journey.

They had both been impressed with the Halls, the bedroom was clean and cosy with an ensuite and the shared kitchen large and modern. The next hour was spent struggling from the car and into the lift with endless boxes and bags, but it felt like they were on holiday, or setting off on an adventure, they giggled as they made the bed and lay side by side to try it out. Then back to the car to find a supermarket and stock up with food; pasta, cereals, milk, bread, butter, yogurt, more and more bags.

By the time they arrived back at the Halls and started to unload the food into the kitchen, the three other girls and their families were all doing the same. They were strangers, different backgrounds, different upbringings, different personalities but all looking for the same thing, to find their place in this new world, to make new friends and create a little family unit of their own.

The other parents were all in couples and somewhat older

than Jen. One set of parents had obviously been through all of this before and suggested that both the girls and their parents had each of the girls' mobile phone numbers in case of emergencies. On one of the walls they fixed a laminated notice containing all of the telephone numbers the girls may possibly need, ranging from the university administration office to a local dentist. They had brought a tin can crusher, industrial sized dustbin bags, a first aid kit and enough cleaning products to last them for the year. They had name stickers on all of their daughter Melissa's belongings and had stocked her designated shelf of the freezer with individual homemade meals.

Jen imagined that Melissa may have been slightly embarrassed by this demonstration of control, but surprisingly she just sat on a stool in the kitchen smiling placidly while her parents organised her new life. Perhaps she was just grateful not to have to worry about the minor details. Or was she, Jen wondered, patiently waiting for them to go, counting down the last few minutes of their authority, biding her time until they at last walked out of the door and she could be free of them. Perhaps she had been planning this escape for years and was now smugly savouring the bitter sweetness of these last few moments before her liberation.

Another couple had brought bottles of champagne, they boisterously told the gathering that they were happily celebrating their freedom as Evie was the last of their four to fly the nest. Now at last the two of them would have their lives back, they could downsize their home, enjoy more holidays, take up new hobbies. Evie listened to all of this with good humour, laughing along with them. She was a very pretty, polished, tall blond, exuding all the confidence and coolness a wealthy and secure upbringing bestows. She already knew her place in the world, already knew herself to be worthy of only the very best things that life would surely offer her. It was by far their most valuable gift to their daughter, thought Jen.

The fourth girl to share the apartment was Jessica, or Jezza as she wanted to be known, another art student, not that you would need to be
 told, her hair was cropped short and spiky, a bright white blond with pink tips. She wore ripped, baggy dungarees, a hand printed t-shirt and loud handmade jewellery. She had piercings in her nose, eyebrows and ears and complex tattoos on the top of her arm, wrists and back of her neck. She was small, pretty and fearless, Jen was relieved that she really liked them all and would have no worries about Lolly fitting in.

There was a party atmosphere in the kitchen, but gradually one by one the parents left until she was the last. For a crazy moment she wondered if she could possibly stay the night and share Laura's bed, but she knew that was ridiculous. She must leave, let the girls enjoy their first evening and celebrate the start of their new adventure.
 She went back to Laura's room for her handbag; she had bought her a special card, full of all the words a mother wants to say to a daughter at a time like this, of love and pride. She had intended to place it on Laura's pillow for her to find when she went to bed, but now she felt a little embarrassed to leave it, it felt inappropriate, too self-indulgent.

Laura did not need reassuring or soothing. She was not going to spend a lonely night in her room, in her bed, missing home. She would be with her new friends, they were already making plans to visit the campus bar later that evening. This was great, this was all Jen had hoped for and worked for. Leave her to it, do not ruin it for her with feelings of guilt, that would be just awful.

Laura had a whole new exciting life starting here and she would simply have to accept that she was not a part of it. It was a new beginning for Laura and some kind of an ending for her, but there was no other solution. Did she want Lolly stuck at home with her, never fulfilling her potential? Of course not, she had worked too hard and sacrificed too much to let her down now.

She could feel the blackness rising up within her, the tightness in her chest, her stomach tying itself into knots. Calm, be calm, remember to breathe and smile, breathe and smile. Look Laura in the eyes or she will know something is wrong, they knew each other too well to be fooled easily. Jen stood in the bedroom for a moment composing herself, breathing deeply, fingers nails pushed into her palms to avoid any tears before she opened the door. She could hear the girls laughing in the kitchen and wished that she could leave without saying goodbye, just slip out, but that was ridiculous, she was the adult here for goodness sake.

She opened the door to the kitchen and smiling brightly said her goodbyes telling the girls how lovely it was to meet them all. Laura walked with her to the front door, held her tightly, thanked her for everything and told her how much she would miss her. For a moment it occurred to Jen that maybe Laura was no different to Melissa. Maybe she too had been suffocated and restrained by her over bearing love and need all of her life and was thankful that she was now just a step away from being unshackled, maybe in reality she couldn't wait for Jen to be gone.

The journey home had been awful, she was numb, lost, her thoughts returning to those dark corners, the black beast heavy on her shoulders, weighing her down and gnawing in her ears.

CHAPTER 2

The plan had always been for Laura to return home for
one weekend each month, but after just two weeks this
plan was scuppered when she was offered a position
working all day Saturday, and Sunday afternoons at an art
gallery. They had both agreed that it would be for the best
if Laura found part time work while studying, offering her
extra spending money. Since she was sixteen Laura had
worked at the local garden centre at weekends and school
holidays, she liked to earn her own money and was aware
of their financial restrictions, they had all they needed but
compared to wealthier friends it was not a lot.
They were both delighted that she had not only been
offered a position so quickly, but one that was perfect for
her. The sacrifice was that she would not be returning
home again until Christmas.
For Jen, this meant that rather than looking forward to
Laura being home once a month, the autumn had seemed a
slow endless drag of dark grey days and darker nights.
'Why don't you come here for a few days instead' Laura
had asked 'There are plenty of cheap hotels or bed and
breakfasts you could stay at'
Although this offer was tempting Jen knew that Laura
would be working, did she really want her there? Did she
hear something contrary in her voice?

'No don't worry, you are so busy and I have quite a lot happening over the next few weekends anyway. It will be Christmas before we know it and I will see you then"
'Are you sure? You are not just saying that are you, I hate to think of you on your own'
'No honestly I am fine, Fliss is missing the boys and has decided to boss me about instead, I don't think there is a weekend she has not planned something'
'Oh, that's good mum'
Laura sounded relieved. Was she a burden to her?
Jen had always struggled, but now the blackness no longer needed to hide, there was no-one to hide from, it crept into her days and was free to torture her nights. Her 'tappings' as Laura called them, whenever she caught her, were once again taking over with a life of their own. She knew that she must fight them back into their ugly, shameful corner, must take back control before Lolly came home, if she saw her like this she would be worried.

The tappings were always present, she could not remember when they started but she was very young. There could be blissful periods when they were hardly noticeable, or even completely forgotten, but there were many times that they ruled her life. They could take control of her whole day, then everything had to be scheduled around them. They were a last defence against the black intrusive thoughts. A pattern that if implemented correctly would shield them both, keeping them safely through another day, another night.

The one, two, three, fours were taking over again. Four taps on each door she closed, four attempts at putting her cup down perfectly, four taps of her fingers together in time with four breathes to push away the dark thoughts. There were four checks that the taps were turned off, her keys were in her pocket, the kettle was unplugged, her handbrake was up, her phone switched on.

It went on and on and on, the more she fought against the knowingly irrational urges, the higher her anxiety, but if she let them take over completely, she would not function at all. It was a constant pay off, to keep them safe she had to make sacrifices to the altar of her OCD but bargained for compromises so that she could function day to day.

Her good friends Helen and Fliss had done all they could to support and distract her while Laura was away, they never said anything but were worried about her being on her own, after all, they and Laura were all she really had. Jen was almost certain they did know about her deep anxieties, she felt she covered it up well, one of the compromises to allowing the tappings to possess her was that she could be normal in public.

They knew her too well though and could see she was struggling, they could see it in her eyes, they heard it in her false laughter. It was difficult, Jen was great company, thoughtful, funny and fiercely loyal but there was something fragile about her, there were many no go areas. Even Fliss, who was notoriously nosey, didn't feel comfortable asking any personal questions, she was evasive about her past, always giving the line there was nothing to say, it was just boring.

They would never have expressed that they felt sorry for her being on her own, but she knew they would be watching out for her and had no doubt they were discussing her situation amongst themselves.

Thoughtfully they organised walks, shopping trips, lunches, and evenings in the pub. But Jen went through the motions more for their sake than for her own. In some strange way she wanted to be left alone so that she could spend her time feeling sad and sorry for herself, could plunge into the depths of despair, as if it were a punishment. Her sorrow felt like a personal mission that she needed to trudge through and complete herself, before being allowed to come through to the other side, back into the light, a creature hibernating alone, waiting for the spring.

Of course, she could not explain her feelings without sounding desperate or pathetic, so instead she smiled, chatted, joked and gossiped just as they would have expected and wanted her to. As often as she could though, she made excuses of being too busy to see them and tried to be left alone.

She was grateful to her friends but her real saviour was Muffin who never left her side, seemingly able to read her moods better than anyone. When she was struggling to cope he would come and sit on her feet, put his chin on her and look deep into her eyes, or jump onto the sofa and lay as closely to her as he possibly could, cuddling him was a great comfort.

Laura had always been affectionate, even now as an adult, she loved to cuddle up on the sofa when they were watching television together and never failed to hug and kiss when she was leaving to go anywhere. Jen missed that physical human contact, but Muffin was a great stand-in. Her days were a ritual of work, walking Muffin and filling the rest of her time with mindless tasks.

She did not even enjoy reading at the moment, normally a passion, instead she spent hours slumped in front of forgetful television programmes, any brain numbing distraction a much appreciated gift. She felt detached, lost from the world, life was passing her by and she really didn't care that it was, the more quickly the days passed, the better.

The highlights were the messages and calls from Laura, her mobile phone never leaving her side. While they were talking all was well, Laura was safe, she was having a wonderful time and enjoying every moment. Her excitement and enthusiasm bubbled over into their conversations, and Jen happily and gratefully played the role of proud, happy, fulfilled mum beautifully.

Christmas had always been a special time in their little family, and they had established many of their own traditions over the years, but this time, of course, Jen had been left to organise everything herself. Previously they would go for walks in the woods and collect ivy, dried hops, holly, and a yule log to decorate the cottage. They made their own scented candles, and always had a special advent one burning in the hearth. Lights were draped over cupboards, the mantlepiece and window frames, the kitchen rich with the smells of the season, as they made their own Christmas puddings, cake, biscuits, mince pies and mulled wine.

At the beginning of December, another annual tradition was the Christmas shopping day with Fliss and Helen in Boughton. For years the three of them had shopped for presents together and enjoyed lunch at their favourite restaurant, The Orchard House. Over the years Laura's gifts had changed from toys and games to more practical presents, clothes, books, make up and jewellery. This year of course she could not buy too much as Laura would have to carry everything back, so she decided on a pair of fluffy slippers that looked like brown bears, that she knew she would love, a bottle of her favourite perfume, a charm for her bracelet and money to spend.

Although this year felt so different, as the season arrived Jen excitedly planned for Laura's return. She found great comfort counting down the days and fussing about each detail to ensure that everything would be perfect. When the day finally arrived, she awoke early, lit the fire, switched on all of the Christmas lights and left a tray of mince pies warming gently in the oven before leaving for the station. She stood watching for the first glimpse of the train coming into sight, and suddenly there she was, laden with bags and her huge backpack. She had rushed into Jen's arms dropping everything onto the floor.

'Wow, what shade are we calling this?' asked Jen, leaning back to admire her new hair colour.

'Its violet' said Laura, proudly turning her head from side to side. 'Do you like it?'

'I love it, but you could have warned me, you are going to clash with my colour scheme'

'Oh mum it's so lovely to be home' she said hugging her

16

tightly again 'I hadn't realised how much I was missing everything, especially how much I was missing you'
'I missed you too my darling, come on lets get you home'
As soon as they stepped in the door of the cottage, it was as if they had never been apart, those long months alone and lonely, were forgotten. Jen made mugs of chai tea, placed the warmed and gooey mince pies on plates and they sat in the sitting room in front of the fire in their rightful places where they had always been and the order of her world was once again restored.

A few years ago Jen had read a self-help book that advised to always try to live in the present, this would help stop the horrors of the past and fears for the future. One of the ways it suggested to do this was when good things happened in your life, when there were moments of pure happiness, you had to briefly pause, freeze the time frame and acknowledge that feeling.

You seized that moment of bliss so that you were aware of all the good times in your life as they happened. It was important to know that even the darkest of days could have glimpses of light. The book suggested the best way to register these moments was to be mindful of that scene. Acting as if your eyes were the lens and your mind the camera, photograph that moment, capture it and store it in your heart.

This was one of those times. As she sat listening to Laura excitedly talking about a Christmas party at the gallery the day before, Jen captured this perfect moment and filed it away in her heart. Live for the moment and appreciate every second of happiness, the book had said, she did try to follow this advice, although it was sometimes difficult to notice any highs within the lows.

They had a wonderful Christmas together as always, enjoying their favourite food, long walks with Muffin, visits to and from friends, games and the customary music and films. Most of the time it was just the two of them, as it had forever been just the two of them. That had always seemed enough, it was certainly enough for Jen, but of course now she understood that Laura needed more, she deserved more. When she chatted about her new life it was obvious that she had already made that leap, spread her wings and discovered that there was much more to life than their little nest.

The two weeks of having Laura at home flew by and suddenly the dreaded day was here. The return journey to the train station, and the goodbyes. Laura had seemed restless over the last few days and Jen realised, a little sadly, that she was excited to be leaving again. Who could blame her? How could Long Bridge compare to city life when you are 18, everything is new and you lived your life without fear.

That night Jen lay for hours in bed unable to sleep, the following morning still dark when she awoke. She listened to the rain pounding on the slate roof and wished she could just stay in bed, just stay right there and sleep, hibernate until Laura returned again. But that was not possible, she had to get back to her normal Monday routine, had to go through the motions of living a normal life.

She left the cottage at 9am, locking her door and checking it four times, walked across the driveway, opening a small wrought iron gate in the wall and followed the gravel path to the back door of Millstone House, unlocking it and turning the door handle four times. She entered the kitchen and switched the kettle on to boil, made a pot of tea then ensuring that everything needed for the wooden tray was perfectly in place, carried it out of the glazed kitchen doors, through the tiled hallway and into the drawing room.

CHAPTER 3

'Good morning' said Jen, as brightly as she could.

Mrs Pendlehurst was sat straight backed in her favourite armchair reading the newspaper. As always, she was smartly dressed, tweed skirt, cream blouse, brown cardigan, her long grey hair neatly pinned back in a bun.

'Good morning dear'

'Did you have a good Christmas?' asked Jen, laying the tea tray on the side table.

'Yes, it was quiet, just the three of us, but very pleasant. The taxi was a little delayed on Saturday, meaning I didn't arrive home until quite late, so thank you for turning up the heating and leaving the fresh groceries, it was most welcome'

'No problem at all'

'I do hope you and Laura enjoyed the Christmas holiday'

'Yes, thank you, we had a lovely time, the only problem was that it all went far too quickly'

'Sadly, the best times in life always do' replied Mrs Pendlehurst gently, 'But before you know it Easter will be here, and Laura will be back'

'Yes, I know'

'Now my dear, I have a church committee meeting at 10 o'clock this morning and at 11.30 someone is coming here to discuss the new plans I have for the garden. I should be back in plenty of time, but if I am running a little late would you please explain that I will not be long and just ask them to wait for me.'

'Yes, of course, I will listen out for them'

After her tea Mrs Pendlehurst collected the necessary paperwork into her old brown leather briefcase, put on her sensible winter boots, wax jacket, wax rain hat and left the house to walk the two hundred yards down the lane to the parish church, Saint Bartholomew's.

Jen worked three mornings a week at Millstone House, cleaning, cooking, laundry, and shopping. Many people would have found her work a mindless task, tedious and repetitive, but Jen thrived on routine and had always enjoyed cleaning, she liked order and tidiness, so it suited her. Even as a child everything had to be in its rightful place.

She also loved every inch of the elegant old house, Mrs Pendlehurst was fond of saying that owners were merely the custodians of houses like these. Jen was neither owner nor custodian, but still enjoyed caring for Millstone.

She worked less hours now than when she first started eighteen years ago. At that time Mr Pendlehurst was still alive and the couple received more visitors. Realistically she could have completed all of her tasks in half the hours she worked, but she stretched them out over the three mornings, partly because she didn't want Mrs Pendlehurst to think that she was not doing her job properly and partly because it filled her own expanse of time.

The position had fitted in perfectly with the needs of a young child. It had been very easy to bring Laura to work with her before she started school, and of course their little cottage was a godsend.

As Laura grew older and no longer needed supervising, Jen knew she should have looked for something more challenging, or perhaps have gone back to college part time to try to build some sort of career for their future. Maybe she had just been lazy, and not made the best use of the last few years, or maybe she was too comfortable in their little world and unsure if she could realistically achieve anything else.

Although she was very aware that the day would come when she may regret not planning ahead, there would inevitably come a time when she would no longer be needed at Millstone. Then she would have to find other employment, not to mention somewhere else for them to live. She realised that she was burying her head in the sand, but had always clung to the hope that when that day came, Laura would be old enough to no longer need her, that she may even by then have a family of her own.

Her main excuse for not planning ahead was that the years had just slipped by so quickly, which they truly had, plus she found it difficult to look too far ahead, more because of fear than naivety. She knew her strengths and weaknesses and the weaknesses seemed to far outweigh the strengths. She had no skills, she was reasonably bright but had missed years of education, added to the fact that she felt a little awkward with new people and new situations. Besides, they had always loved it here, this was their home, she honestly couldn't imagine being anywhere else now.

Mrs Pendlehurst did not do domestic, she disliked cooking and housework, her greatest love being the extensive gardens that she had shaped over the last 40 years. No matter what the weather, she was happiest working outside or in the greenhouse, so was grateful to be able to leave everything to Jen. Their relationship had always been respectful, but it had never crossed the line between employer, employee into a friendship. Mrs Pendlehurst had always lived with staff and was very comfortable with the etiquette of their relationship, both its courtesies and boundaries.

Apart from the assigned hours that Jen worked, their paths hardly crossed. In fact, Mrs Pendlehurst had only been inside the cottage twice in over eighteen years. The first time was the day that Jen had arrived at Millstone House and the second the day that Mr Pendlehurst had died. There was no doubt in Jen's mind that Mrs Pendlehurst was thankful to have her here, particularly since the sudden death of her husband 16 years ago. Although at the beginning there had been some difficult adjustments for them both and it had taken time for Jen to feel a valued part of the household, now after all these years there was now a clear understanding of mutual trust and respect.

It had been late spring when Jen and Laura first arrived at Millstone. The Pendlehursts had fortunately for them needed a new housekeeper suddenly and with some urgency when their employees, The Attley's, had left them quite abruptly after being with them for over 20 years. They had been shocked that Eva Attley their wonderful cook and housekeeper, and her husband Bill, who worked in the garden, could just abandon them with so little prior warning. The couple had very suddenly decided to take early retirement and move to the coast to be near their daughter, and within weeks of their decision they had gone. It had been distressing for Mrs Pendlehurst, and even Mr Pendlehurst, who normally kept his distance from the domestic arrangements, had been surprised by their departure and taken it upon himself to find a replacement, he had even organised for the redecoration of the cottage and the new furnishings. Fortunately, a work colleague was able to highly recommend Jen, and the problem had been solved quickly.

Although there were initial doubts, Jen was so young and had a baby in tow. As Mrs Pendlehurst had shown them around the cottage on that first day, Jen had carried Laura in her arms, silently walking from room to room. By the time they had returned to the kitchen Mrs Pendlehurst had started to feel that it had maybe been a huge mistake hiring somebody without going through an agency. She was noticeably young, was she experienced enough to run a large house? She was also far too quiet, and what would she do with the baby while she was working?

'I am sorry my dear, maybe this was not such a good idea' she started to say, 'The cottage is very small and may not be suitable for you and your daughter, perhaps we should have invited you to view the accommodation before you committed to....'

Jen had interrupted her 'No, this is perfect, we will be really happy here thank you Mrs Pendlehurst'

'Are you sure? The village is rather quiet, you may be lonely. Do your family live far away?'

'No we will be fine thank you, it is everything we could want, I promise I will not let you down'

Jen saw the doubt in Mrs Pendlehursts eyes, but she handed her the keys to the cottage, and invited her to come over to the house if there were any problems. The man who had driven them to Millstone and waited in the car brought in two suitcases, a buggy, a box of books and toys and several carrier bags of food.

'Does the baby not need a cot?' Mrs Pendlehurst had asked

'Oh no, she is fine thank you, she sleeps in with me'

'Oh, I see. Well, I will leave you to settle in and on Monday morning I will show you around the house and we can go through your duties. As I said if there is any problem at all, do come and see me'

Mrs Pendlehurst was not at all convinced that they were making the right decision, but was assured by her husband that Jen came highly recommended by a work colleague, and that if there was any problem at all, they would simply give her notice and find someone else.

On the Monday morning, as arranged, Jen was at Millstone ready for work, Mrs Pendlehurst showed her around the house and explained her duties, she had never been inside such a beautiful home before.

Laura had settled into the routine immediately and never caused any problems, at first she would lay in her buggy or on a blanket playing with her toys watching Jen while she worked. As she grew older she would sit at the kitchen table, drawing or reading.

The Pendlehursts never seemed overly fond of children or even particularly comfortable around them, but they had to admit that the child was never any trouble.

Jen was not afraid of hard work and wanted to please the Pendlehursts. Managing the housework and laundry was easy, but Mrs Attley had been a wonderful cook and at one time the Pendlehursts would entertain friends and business colleagues quite regularly.

Jen's cooking was basic and certainly not of the same standard, even though she always tried her best to follow the recipes in the cookery books in the kitchen, they never came out looking quite the same as the photographs. Occasionally Jen could see that Mrs Pendlehurst was disappointed by her efforts, but Mr Pendlehurst never complained or even commented on the food that was served, he seemed more than happy to be able to hand the domestic arrangements back to his wife without any further suggestions or input.

He was a partner in a large law firm and worked long hours, shortly after their arrival his work schedule meant that he was spending even less time at home during the week and more nights at their apartment in London. Consequently, apart from the annual village choir Christmas drinks party, or an occasional guest, they now rarely entertained at the house.

Jen was more than grateful for the chance of this new life, she had all that she wanted, a safe, peaceful home for Laura and the time to devote to being the best mum she could possibly be. They did not really need anyone nor anything else, they were happy.

They had left the grey tower block with their few possessions very early the morning they had first arrived. Sitting in the back of the car they watched as the concrete inner city flowed into the suburbs and onto the motorway and the motorway onto a duel carriageway and then eventually there was the sign for Long Bridge.

They had entered the village through an avenue of beech trees leading to a stone bridge across the river. Following the road they passed the pond and the village green where children were playing cricket, in front of Saint

Bartholomew's Church, then turned down the lane, and drove through the iron gates of Millstone House with its sentry of huge oak trees. Arriving here had felt like entering a different world, it was a completely different world to the one they had come from, a world Jen was determined they would never return to. Long Bridge was all Jen could have wished for and more, she felt so lucky.

At first Mrs Pendlehurst had managed the weekly shopping herself, but after a few months they had suggested they would pay for Jen to have driving lessons so that she could take over this chore and run other errands that needed doing. Mr Pendlehurst bought his wife a new car so her small hatchback was passed onto Jen. This meant that their weekends could now be spent taking Laura swimming or to the park, and later to the cinema, museums and galleries. Mrs Pendlehurst was a stalwart of the community, governor of the village school, trustee of the church committee, chairperson of the village horticultural society and a member of the local choir. Sadly though, her network of friends in the village had diminished over the years, as growing older tends to dictate. She had always kept herself busy and was a very independent lady, but Jen did wonder if she too was sometimes lonely, although nothing was ever said.

Apart from a younger sister and niece in Lyme Regis whom she visited once or twice a year there was no other close family. Mr Pendlehurst's younger brother, his wife and their son had lived in Canada for more than forty years, although both the brother and his wife had died some time ago. Sometimes Jen thought about the relationship between the two of them, their lives rubbing along together, seemingly independent, but in truth both relying heavily on the other.

CHAPTER 4

It had just started to rain heavily when the bell chimed at the front of the house. Jen opened the panelled door and the cold wind whipped the spray into the porch. The man was dressed in heavy duty waterproofs, from his work boots to the hood of his jacket pulled over a black woollen hat. For a moment he seemed surprised to see Jen, then quickly looked away towards the old Land Rover and the black labrador sat in the passenger seat, watching him intently.

'David Brook' he said without taking his eyes from the vehicle 'I'm here to see Mrs Pendlehurst'.

'Oh yes, sorry she will not be long, would you like to wait in the porch? She will be back soon'

'No, I will wait in the vehicle' he mumbled as he turned back.

'Okay, suit yourself' said Jen under her breath as she closed the door against the storm and went back to the warm kitchen to finish the cottage pie.

A few minutes later she heard Mrs Pendlehurst return and voices in the hallway. By lunch time she was back in her cottage. She lit the kindling in the wood burner and switched on the side lamps, Fliss was calling in for coffee soon and she wanted the cottage to look cosy and welcoming.

Fliss was one of the first people they met when they
moved Long Bridge. Within a few weeks of making the
village their home, Jen had tentatively taken Laura to the
local Mother and Toddler group in the Village Hall at the
suggestion of Mrs Pendlehurst, who was at that time also
on the Village Hall committee.

Fliss was running the group and had swooped on them
from across the room as they had sidled quietly in the
door. Jen still remembers being slightly intimidated as this
larger than life character cornered her as soon as she
arrived, she was tall with long red curly hair, huge smile,
huge breasts.

'Hi, you must be Jen,' she shouted excitedly, huge voice as
well Jen noticed. 'Rosemary Pendlehurst has told me all
about you, I am so glad you have decided to come, and this
must be Laura, oh she is gorgeous, a real poppet. Come on,
follow me and I will introduce you to everyone and get you
a coffee, my name is Fliss, come and sit over here with us'
Jen had obediently followed, she had been so nervous to
come here, nearly turning back twice. This was all new to
her, she had no idea what to expect, or even what they
were meant to do, but she was very aware how important it
was to be a part of the community for Laura's sake if not
her own, she didn't want her to be lonely and isolated
from other children. They both needed to fit into this new
life, and this was a first step.

The other women all seemed very friendly, there were
about twelve mums in the hall, a couple of grandmothers
and more than twenty children up to school age. Laura
enjoyed every moment, loving all the attention she received
from the adults and fascinated by the other children. Jen
was not so comfortable, she sat quietly listening and
smiling, only answering any questions when needed to, she
had already practiced her lines at home. She couldn't help
but glance at the wall clock every few minutes, wishing the
time would go faster so that they could respectfully escape.
The other mums did their best to include her in the

conversations and helpfully offered advice and information about the area. By the end of the session Jen knew all about the village preschool, primary school, the best doctor to see at the surgery, the organic farm shop, nearest swimming pool, baby gym lessons, music sessions, dance classes.

When the morning session came to an end and the families started to leave, to her surprise and slight embarrassment, Fliss hugged and kissed both her and Laura, insisting they come to her house for coffee the following Friday afternoon, it was suggested too quickly to think of an excuse why they could not go, so she agreed.

At that time Fliss lived in a beautiful barn conversion on the outskirts of the village with her husband James, a property developer and their two sons Henry who was four and Hugo two. Her life could have featured in a glossy country magazine, thought Jen. Adoring, successful husband, bright happy children, amazing home, luxury cars, skiing holidays in the winter, a property by the sea for the summer, lots of friends, bags of confidence, and totally comfortable in her own skin.

When Jen arrived with Laura that Friday afternoon, she had presumed it would just be the two of them. She had been nervous about going, practicing in her head possible scenarios, and thinking interesting things that she could talk about if necessary, but apart from having children what on earth did they have in common.

She was relieved when she arrived to see there were already three other mums and their various children sat in the enormous conservatory that also acted as a playroom. Great, now hopefully she could just smile lots and blend into the furniture. Fliss, was the perfect hostess, unflappable amongst the noise and gentle chaos, handing out cups of fresh coffee and biscuits to the mothers and beakers with drinks and tiny cakes to the assortment of children.

These seemed to be a different group of women to those at

the Mother and Toddlers, Jen would soon learn that Fliss had a seemingly endless supply of friends, her home and life overflowing with the people she found. Although even all these years later, Jen was still undecided if Fliss was a flame that people were drawn to, or if she simply needed to collect them all around her.

Again that day Fliss enthusiastically introduced Jen to the rest of the group and found her a seat on the long velvet moss green sofa next to a slim woman with short dark pixie hair, who smiled at Jen and introduced herself quietly as Helen.

Helen had a three year old son Jonathan, forever known as Jonty, and a daughter the same age as Laura, Katie. The two little girls sat propped up on their mother's knees transfixed with each other. At some point that afternoon Fliss had taken a photograph of the girls together which became one of those pictures that happen unnoticed and unimportant at the time, but years later feel like one of the lynchpins of life, as so often our memories are recalled through old photographs imprinted in our minds.

In the photograph the girls are both looking up at Fliss with gummy smiles, their heads touching. In the following years the girls had re-enacted that photograph countless times, Laura even painting a portrait of them in the same pose when they were both sixteen. Looking back they had seemed inseparable from that moment on, in fact the only thing keeping them apart now, was their different choices of universities, Katie was studying veterinary science in Bristol, although they still talked, or messaged each other nearly every day and shared in each other's new lives.

Helen, her husband Mike, Jonty and Katie, lived at their family farm Upper Leys with Mike's parents at that time. The farm was just outside the village and over the years became a second home to them both, in Laura's eyes it was simply heaven. To live in a sprawling farmhouse with acres of land, lots of animals and a big family had been her dream.

Helen was a very keen horse rider, so it was only natural when they were old enough that both girls had ponies,so much of their weekends were spent riding, grooming and mucking out or competing at local gymkhanas. Jen could not have asked for more, Laura she had an idyllic childhood. Any difficult decisions that she may have had to make in the past to get them here, were more than worth it to see her blossom into such a confident young woman.

Fliss and Helen were opposite ends of the spectrum. Fliss always larger than life, loud, generous, warm and charismatic. She loved to be the centre of attention, loved shocking people with her acerbic wit and gutter language and Helen, down to earth, gentle, quiet and thoughtful. Perhaps Jen was the grey between their black and white, she was always grateful for having both of them in her life, and the love and laughter they shared.

CHAPTER 5

The years tumbled by, Laura, like most of the children in the village attended Long Bridge Nursery then moved on to the village school under the sharp eye of the indomitable headmistress Mrs Hough, who had taught many of their parents and even some of their grandparents. Jen and Laura both contentedly fell into the gentle rhythm of village and school life. Easter egg hunts on the village green, May Day Parade, Summer Fete, Harvest Supper, Halloween, Bonfire Night, Christmas carol singing and the New Year lantern walk. Winter snows took the children to Pikes Ridge for the best sledging in the village and summers were spent picnicking, horse riding or playing in the hay barn at Upper Leys Farm.

Fliss and James owned a holiday home by the sea in Dorset where Fliss stayed with her boys for much of the summer school holidays and each year Helen and Jen visited with their three children to stay with them for a week. They were always remembered as idyllic holidays, days on the beach and walks along the cliffs in all weathers, evenings playing games and cooking supper together.

It was all so different to Jen's childhood, and she made sure it was. Sometimes she did feel guilty that Laura didn't have a father to join them at parents' evenings and sports days. There were no grandparents in her life to dote over her, or be there for birthdays and Christmases, no aunts or uncles or cousins to visit and share family memories with, but Laura had never really questioned their absence, she had always seemed contented and happy.

Jen knew that one day questions would have to be answered and skeletons dragged from their cupboards, she just prayed Laura would understand the decisions she had made for them both, and not judge her too harshly.

And now here she was, daydreaming on a wet January afternoon of such happy times, times that she had to face were gone, never to return, life moves on and there is nothing you can do about it. All of the people who had shared those years, had now moved on with their lives except her, she was stagnant, floundering in a muddy swamp with no idea of how to escape and no desire to even start to try. She was glad Fliss was coming today, she needed her today.

She was filling the kettle when there was a knock at the door.

'Come in its open' she called 'when have you ever bothered knocking.....' she giggled turning as the door opened.

She stopped abruptly and caught her breath. For a moment she did not recognise him and was startled, but then realised that in the doorway was David Brook, rain running off his hood and jacket.

'She's had a fall, you had better come and see to her,' he mumbled.

For a moment Jen could not think who he could be talking about.

'What do you mean, is it Mrs Pendlehurst?' She tried to clear her head. 'What's happened?'

'She slipped over, I've taken her into the house, but you had better come and see to her' he turned and left.

Jen quickly pulled on her wellington boots and grabbing her raincoat held it over her head before rushing out into the pouring rain. Running up the path to the kitchen door of Millstone, she saw David Brook already outside waiting for her, as she approached he opened the door and held it while she passed. Mrs Pendlehurst was sat on a kitchen chair looking disheveled, pale, and rather embarrassed.

'Mrs P are you alright, whatever happened?'
Jen crouched down next to her.
'Yes dear, I am perfectly all right, I have simply slipped and must have twisted my ankle, I am sure it will be absolutely fine, I don't know what all the fuss is about.' She sighed loudly 'Now if you would just kindly help me into the drawing room, I am sure I will be able to manage from there'
She stood unsteadily holding onto the table but flinched when she put her weight onto the already swollen ankle. Without saying a word David Brook removed his sodden jacket and hat, Jen had already noticed he had left his huge muddy work boots at the door. He walked over and gently picked up the elderly lady as easily as if she were a child.
'Which way?' he asked, as he carried an astounded Mrs Pendlehurst out of the room.
Jen hurried in front of them, opening the drawing room door and leading him in. She moved the footstool to beside the favoured armchair and stood back while he gently placed the now flushed and silenced Mrs Pendlehurst onto the chair.
'I will get some ice for your ankle and make you some tea' said Jen,
She turned to David Brook 'Would you like some tea?'
'No thanks, I've got to go, I'm already late' he answered without looking at her.
'If the weather is okay Mrs Pendlehurst, I'll be back sometime next month as arranged, I will let you know'
With that he walked briskly back to the kitchen in his woollen socks to retrieve his outer clothes. Jen decided to make herself busy and hopefully waste a little time by finding a blanket to place over Mrs Pendlehurst's knees and a few suitable cushions to put behind her back, making sure he had plenty of time to leave the house before she returned to the kitchen.

She was not sure if he had some kind of personality disorder, was painfully shy or just plain rude, but whatever was wrong with him, he was not a comfortable person to be around.

When she eventually walked out through the hallway a little while later, she heard voices. Fliss. She had forgotten all about her. Jen opened the glazed door to find her sat on the kitchen table with her feet up on one of the dining chairs and David Brook stood at the back door putting his boots on. She was busy entering his telephone number into her mobile phone and giggling.

'Oh here you are' she said as Jen walked into the kitchen 'I couldn't find anyone, but David has been filling me in' She looked at David and gave him one of her dazzlers as Jen called them.

'Poor old Mrs P, is she okay?'

'Yes, I think she is fine, just a little shaken'

'Oh dear, I will pop in and see her'

She slipped gracefully down from the table and sauntered towards the hallway door, opening it she turned and looked back at David, tossing her red locks over her shoulder and thrusting her ample chest to look its best.

'Bye David don't you forget to make some time for me, I am not easily dissuaded you know. I'll come and track you down' she giggled as she shut the door behind her.

Jen turned silently to fill the kettle and without another word he was gone.

She made tea for the three of them and wrapping a small bag of frozen peas in a tea towel carried it all on a tray into the sitting room. Fliss was crouched on the floor next to Mrs Pendlehurst's chair leaning on the armrest chatting animatedly and the two of them were laughing.

Jen was always aware that she was an employee and had never expected to have an intimate or even close relationship with her employer, in fact, she preferred to keep some distance. But she always felt a small pang of jealously at the way Fliss so easily managed to charm everyone. She had the ability to make anyone feel special, the most important person in the room, the centre of her world. Jen loved her and would not have wanted to change anything about her. She knew that the problem lay with her, but sometimes Fliss's easy charm was a sharp reminder of her own inadequacies.

'Oh here you are' said Fliss 'Come and sit down'

She jumped to her feet and taking the tray from Jen put it on the coffee table before taking charge of the ice pack and gently holding it on Mrs Pendlehurst's ankle.

'I have just been trying to discover the secret of how Mrs P managed to entice David Brook to come and work here. What has she got, that the rest of us haven't?'

'I have assured Fliss,' said Mrs Pendlehurst 'that my only appeal to Mr Brook is the three-acre walled garden. I am afraid the days when I may have been able to entice any man have long gone, if they even ever existed'

'Don't you believe it Mrs P you are still a very attractive woman, you know as well as I do how much Old Harry the milkman hankers after you' teased Fliss

'Oh, my goodness' laughed Mrs Pendlehurst, 'He must be ninety-five and has been married four times.'

'I have seen the way he looks at you, obviously desperate to whisk you away and make you his lucky Mrs number five'

'You are a dreadful person mocking a poor old lady with a twisted ankle unable to defend herself'

'What's so special about David Brook?' interrupted Jen sitting down opposite them

'You don't know about David Brook!' gasped Fliss dramatically. 'You must have noticed the Robinsons garden, down Ponds Reach'

'Yes, of course I have,' said Jen 'I often walk Muffin through that way, it looks amazing now.'

'That was David Brooks design'

'Oh, that's where I know him from, I thought he looked familiar, he was there with a couple of other men working on the garden last year'

'He was also in The Plough' said Fliss 'at my birthday bash, I remember pointing him out to you'

'Did you? I am surprised you remember anything about that evening at all, I just remember having to get you home.'

'No, not my best night. Anyway, apparently as I am sure I told you at the time, he moved into Meadow Farm over the other side of Bellwick a few years ago and started some sort of specialist nursery. He's quite well known and has worked on some celebrity's gardens, featured on television gardening programmes and in magazines, he won gold at Chelsea a couple of times too. A very few lucky people have managed to persuade him to take on their garden projects, but he is very picky, he has totally ignored my enquiries for his services in the past'

'Why would you need your garden landscaped?' It's nearly all courtyard'

'Oh, I am sure I could find something for him to do'

'Oh, dear Mrs P time to cover your ears, as usual I must apologise for my friend'

'But didn't you notice his hands?' continued Fliss, now in full dramatic flow 'Such big strong hands, and he's so……earthy'

'Felicity Cooper' exclaimed Mrs Pendlehurst 'I think we have gone quite far enough with that conversation'

'Yes, quite right' said Jen 'Time for me to take her and that mouth away. Come on you, come and help me in the kitchen, I will get your lunch ready Mrs P.'

They went through and Jen started sweeping the dried mud left from David's boots.

'You are dreadful, you are going to make her blood pressure go up' laughed Jen, 'Did you not see how flushed she was?'

'She was not flushed, she was blushing, if you ask me, she'd had exactly the same thoughts as me about those big hands. She's not that old you know, she's not dead.'

'Honestly, you are seriously going to have to find yourself another man, you are starting to dribble every time you get near one'

'To be truthful I don't know what I want. You know me, I love to flirt but I wouldn't want to get in a situation like James again'

'They can't all be like him'

'Hopefully not, and it has been sodding ages, there is just no one around here that interests me, and there is no one at work. Well, nobody I've not tried already. David Brook is fresh blood, a new project that I could get my teeth into and my legs around'

'Well, you managed to prise his telephone number out of him, why don't you ring him and suggest something. Ha, who am I preaching to? You know all the tricks, he doesn't stand a chance.'

'No, it's no good, I tried all my best moves and I didn't get any response from him at all. He made it plainly obvious that he wasn't interested, I must be losing it. They say as you get older you become invisible to men, something to do with our hormones or sex pheromones or something'

Fliss sighed 'And it must be true, you watch when a ripe young women walks into a room, even if they have their backs to her, men instinctively look around, there simply must be a young and fertile scent. That used to happen when I walked into a room, but not anymore'

She sat on a chair at the kitchen table, her chin resting in her hands, in full sulk mode.

'Yes they do turn around to see you, they may not smell you, but they can't help hearing you'

'Bitch'

Jen gave her a hug

'Listen, there is not a man alive who could possibly deserve you'

'Ah, that's nice, if a load of bollocks. No it's too late for me now, I must obviously be oozing an "I am 'past it' aroma".

I may as well have it tattooed across my forehead, not that anyone would notice. It's all down to nature you know, once we are menopausal, women are only still on this earth to help their grandchildren survive, then we have fulfilled our destiny, that's it for us until we keel over and die. Life really is shit'

'I don't know what happened to my pheromones then' laughed Jen gently stroking her long red curls hair away from her face, as she would have a child.

'I must have missed that phase altogether, I think I have always been pretty invisible. Anyway, I doubt very much that he did not notice you, you don't exactly do subtle with that teeth, tits and hair flicking routine. You most probably scared the life out of him, poor chap"

"Oh, I don't know" Fliss sighed

You can't be that desperate anyway, you are far too good for him. I don't know what you even see in him to be honest. I think there is something a bit strange about him, he is either incredibly rude or simply weird in some way. I hate it when people don't give you any eye contact'

'Eye contact? No, that wasn't the problem, he looked into my eyes okay. The trouble was he just looked bored and his eyes did not stray down once. Oh, I'm sorry, I am meant to be here cheering you up, not whinging'

"You always cheer me up" said Jen giving her another hug "lets sort out Mrs P and get some coffee"

They spent the rest of the afternoon together, checking in on Mrs Pendlehurst and catching up with all the gossip. Fliss was always great company, it was rare for her to be unhappy, even though she had been through a lot in the last few years. She always managed to see the funny side of things, especially when they were to do with herself.

When Jen had first met Fliss, she had imagined that her life was perfect, but it is true that you never know what is really going on within other people's marriages. Six years ago, the illusion was ripped apart.

It had been an awful start to the year for Fliss. Her mother who lived in London, had suffered a stroke in the January, so she had spent much of her time travelling back and forth to the hospital. Her friends rallied around, making sure the boys were looked after, helping with meals and shopping, but of course she was exhausted.

Her parents had divorced a number of years before, but she had always been very close to her father who lived in the next village, so it was a terrible shock when a few months later one of his neighbours found him dead after a heart attack.

Her mother had by that time been discharged from hospital and moved into a care home, but she then sadly also died in the May. The stress and exhaustion of organising both of her parent's funerals and sorting out their belongings and properties had really taken its toll on poor Fliss, but slowly her life started getting back to normal.

Then in the July it became clear that James's business was having problems. Fliss was obviously worried, James had lost a substantial amount of money through several bad investments and although eventually Fliss would benefit from her parent's estates, that money was not yet available. What troubled her more was that James seemed to have simply given up trying and spent less and less time at his office. Instead he moped about their house all day watching television and drinking.

She thought that he must be suffering with stress or depression and worried that he may be going through some kind of midlife crisis or even a breakdown, but he denied there was a problem and refused to seek help. They were constantly arguing and the tension in their home could be unbearable at times, both being such fiery characters.

Although she did not say it, Jen wondered if some of their problems may be because they were not used to spending so much time together.

James normally worked long hours and was often away from home because of his business, at weekends he played golf or went fishing or shooting. The only time they really spent together as a family was during their holidays.

One day Jen called at their house to return some books she had borrowed. James answered the door and seemed overly cheerful, making her wonder if he had been drinking even though it was only 11 o'clock in the morning. He insisted that she come in as Fliss would be home any minute and would be disappointed to have missed her. She had not planned to stay but did not want to seem rude, so she followed James into the kitchen and accepted his offer of coffee.

He chatted while he made their drinks, immediately making her sense that something seemed wrong. He was normally rather a serious man, more a type of man's man really, certainly not comfortable with female small talk. In fact in all the years they had known each other, Jen could not think of any other time they had even really talked, they had certainly never been alone, and yet here he was laughing and chatting and yes, she was sure she wasn't imagining it, flirting.

'That's a lovely jumper you're wearing' he said putting her coffee on the table and taking the seat next to her.

'I have had it for years' Jen said, instinctively putting her arms protectively around her waist.

'Well, that's the thing about you, with your body you look good in anything'

Jen physically cringed 'James I don't think you should be talking like that, I know you are just teasing but you are embarrassing me'

'I am not teasing, I have always fancied you, always wanted to have you. Come on, let me see you' he leaned over and tried to move her arms away from her body.

'James, stop it,' she said pulling away from him 'Fliss will be home any minute. What the hell are what are you doing?'

'She's not coming back for the rest of the day' laughed James 'But I have you here to play with now, come on, it's just a bit of fun, no one will know'.

Jen jumped up and grabbing her jacket and handbag rushed out of the house without another word. Even when she slammed the door behind her she could still hear him laughing.

For the rest of the day it was all she could think about, she felt physically sick. There had always been something about him that she did not particularly like, he could be quite arrogant and moody at times. She had always thought that Fliss was far too good for him but would never have said anything.

Until the sad events of the last six months, Fliss had always seemed happy with her life, she had certainly never seriously spoken about any problems in their relationship, just the normal wifely grumbles.

She had seemed to be contented, undoubtedly enjoying all the comfortable trappings of a middle-class wife and mother. She had never had to work or worry about money, they had a wonderful home and the children, whom she adored, attended a particularly good private school. James had always worked long hours, so she had made her own life and circle of friends and seemed to be fulfilled.

Jen played the scene in her head over and over, again and again; she kept wondering what had prompted his behaviour. She was entirely sure though that she had done nothing to encourage him. Maybe he had been drinking, or maybe Fliss was right and he was having some kind of breakdown.

Could she have handled the situation differently? She did not know. Should she tell Fliss? She did not know that either. The last thing she wanted to do was hurt her or the boys and put them through even more trauma.

She had a sleepless night, one minute deciding that she must tell her, that is what she would have wanted after all,

and the following minute changing her mind and hoping
that she had misread his actions. When she arrived home
the next day from Millstone she was disturbed to see
James's car pulling up outside the cottage. For a moment
she thought twice about opening the door, but he would
have known she was there, her car was parked outside, and
the cottage windows were open. She decided she was being
ridiculous, overreacting, he was just James, her friends'
husband. Probably here to apologise and beg her not to tell
Fliss.

'What do you want James?' she asked, holding the door
half open, hopefully letting him know he was not welcome
in.

'I need to talk to you' he replied curtly

'What about? What have you got to say?'

'Can't I come in and talk, instead of standing here on your
doorstep like a stranger?'

'I am about to go out' she lied 'Just say what you have
come here for'

'Just let me in for five minutes. You're not scared of me,
are you?'

His look of disbelief made her feel a little ashamed of her
misgivings and she hesitantly opened the door and stepped
aside. He walked into the kitchen and leaned back against
the work tops.

'Look, about yesterday' he said 'I am sorry if you think I
put you in an awkward position'

'Awkward position!' Jen repeated 'So you should be sorry,
it is bad enough for you to behave in that way towards
anybody, but to act like that with one of your wife's friend
is disgusting, whatever has got into you?'

He laughed softly 'I haven't come here to apologise if that's
what you're thinking. The fact is I was telling the truth, I
have always fancied you, I am hoping its true what they say
about the quiet ones. Look, just forget about Fliss she
never needs to know, it will be our little secret. We are all
adults, and you won't be the first you know.'

He saw the shock on Jen's face

'Yes, there have been other women. I honestly do not know if my darling wife is too stupid to realise, or just conveniently turns a blind eye, or perhaps she simply doesn't give a shit. Whichever way it is, I am not happy with her anymore, have not been for a long time now, she bores me'

'How dare you speak about her like that in front of me. She is my friend, and the mother of your children, you callous bastard. I have always known that she is far too good for you, you are lucky to have her.'

He took a step across the kitchen and for one moment she thought he was going to hit her, but he pushed her back, pinning her with his weight against the door.

'You act innocent, but I know where you are from and what you really are' he whispered into her ear, his breath pungent with alcohol.

He pushed his mouth onto hers, his unshaven face rough against her skin. For a moment she froze, and he slid his hands under her sweatshirt.

Instinct suddenly kicked in. Forcing her arms free she wildly clawed at his face with both hands, aiming for his eyes. He gasped and jumped back.

'You little bitch' he hissed

Jen slipped away from him and snatching a bread knife from the draining board held it front of her.

'Get the fuck out of my house'

He stared at her for a moment, blood starting to seep from the scratches on his face.

'Don't think I won't use this'

He hesitated and looked at the knife, there was something about her voice, her face, that convinced him.

'What's wrong with you, can't you take a joke, you're a fucking mad woman. I want you to keep away from my wife and children, do you hear me'

She took a step towards him, knife if front of her 'Get out of my house'

He slammed the door on his way out and drove off.

Jen dropped the knife, her whole body shaking uncontrollably, the terror of being so vulnerable flooding over her. Paralysing fear she thought she would never face again, certainly not here.

Sometimes in life we are faced with the dilemma of having to hurt the people we love, she already knew that. Now there was no other choice, James had made the decision for her, he was unworthy of Fliss and the boys, and a danger to their future.

Another reason for her decision was she knew that James had persuaded Fliss to invest her inheritance money into a new business venture. No, she had to tell her immediately. Her hands were shaking as she called her mobile which went straight to voicemail.

'This is Jen; I don't know where you are or what you are doing but I need to see you as soon as possible. Please don't panic, I am fine, the boys are fine, but I need to talk to you urgently. Don't go home first. Sorry to sound so weird but please Fliss just trust me.'

Within the hour Fliss had arrived. Jen had spent the whole time rehearsing her speech, over and over again but in the end all she could do was hug Fliss as she walked in the door and blurt out what had happened over the last two days.

Fliss was incredibly calm, in fact totally out of character. Jen had been unsure how she would react to the news that the man she was married to and the father of her children, was a serial cheat and liar. She had expected her to be furious, if not hysterical, she never once imagined this total composure.

It was almost as if Fliss had been cruising along in her marriage, preparing for an iceberg, and she was ready. Jen decided James must have been right, somewhere deep down Fliss must have known what he was really like. Did she even know about the other women?

Fliss was the last woman on earth that Jen could imagine putting up with that type of marriage, a relationship that was just a sham, but in the end we all do the best we can with what life throws at us. Eventually most of us have to compromise with what we really want in our lives against what we have been given.

You never can predict how someone will react to a situation no matter how well you know them. Maybe she had wanted to protect the children or maybe she had put up with the relationship to maintain her lifestyle; probably she had wanted to safeguard both.

But now the blinkers had been ripped off and there was no going back, no blissful ignorance, no reconciliation, she seemed already resolved to the fact that it was now time to face up to the realities and move things along.

So again, that year Fliss had more than her share of stress and sorrow, but she handled the whole episode with steely determination. Within six months the family home had been sold and James had moved back to Edinburgh. Fliss purchased a pretty thatched cottage in the village for her and the boys and they seemed to quickly settle.

It was no longer the life they had been used to financially, but they still had everything they needed. It had been normal for James to be away often, so his absence had been easy to adjust to and Fliss now worked part time as an events coordinator for a charity, which suited her perfectly. Her social life was still very full with many friends, although she had immediately noticed that far fewer invitations came your way once you were single, from those friends who were couples.

It was as if only even numbers fitted into plans for dinner parties, skiing trips or weekends away. Were they worried that it may be awkward, and you would end up on your own in a corner? Or did they feel that without a partner you could not possibly have anything in common with those who had been blessed enough to have kept theirs?

Or maybe it was the old adage of being cautious about inviting a single woman, would they be prowling the room ready to pounce on one of your men and steal them away? They were closer since the marriage break up. Even though quite different, they were comfortable together, could chat for hours and literally fall about with laughter over the silliest things. Laura often teased them about having never grown up, but no matter what your age, having a friend you can really laugh with is something special.

Fliss was a bit lost at the moment, Henry was on a gap year, he had already been travelling for two months in Australia and was now continuing through Asia until June. Hugo was in the second year of his engineering degree and on a placement year in California.

As usual, she had of course put on her bravest face, making jokes about how at last she would have the house to herself and the endless passionate trysts she would be able to enjoy, but Jen knew it was all bravado. It made her grateful that however much she was missing Laura, at least she was just a few hours away.

CHAPTER 6

Jen stayed at Millstone for most of the day and returned in the evening to help Mrs Pendlehurst up the stairs. Although she was dismissed once they had managed the last step.

'Thank you, I am quite capable on my own from here, good night, be sure to lock up properly'

This episode made Jen once again consider what would happen if the time came that Mrs Pendlehurst could no longer live independently. Would she need to have a full time carer or move to a care home? Either of those options would inevitably mean she lost her home.

The next morning, she was pleased and relieved to see Mrs Pendlehurst almost back to normal mobility, her ankle now just slightly swollen. Good, life back to normal, all those decisions and dark thoughts could be filed away for another time, she can get on with today.

Although feeling much better, Mrs Pendlehurst had decided that she needed to take things easy for the rest of the day, so she was at her desk, leg up on a footstool catching up with her paper work and correspondence when the doorbell rang. Jen put down the laundry basket and opened the front door to David Brook.

'I was just passing and thought I would check that everything was okay'

It was raining heavily again but he didn't have his hat and rain was running down his face and neck. He looked at his boots and then across at his Land Rover.

'Oh yes, her ankle seems to be much better today thank you, do you want me to see if she is up to visitors?'

'No, no, don't disturb her. I can't stop anyway, I was just checking everything was all right, I have something in the truck, I'll leave it out here' and with that he turned and left

Jen waited uncomfortably at the door, what did he mean? Did he want her to wait for him to come back? The rain was blowing into the hallway and it was bitterly cold, so she decided to step back inside and wait behind a crack in the door, in case he knocked again.

She watched him collect something from the Land Rover, carrying it back in his arms and placing it carefully to the side of the door. It was a large terracotta pot that looked so beautiful Jen simply had to open the door again for a better look. It was glorious, a perfect picture of tiny vibrant daffodils, snowdrops, crocuses, and hyacinths in a bed of moss. The pot stood out like precious jewels on a green velvet cushion against the dark and grey of the winter morning.

'Wow,' said Jen 'that is so beautiful.'

She stepped outside forgetting the rain and leaned down to get a closer look.

David leaned down briefly as well to brush a little escaped soil from the rim of the pot.

Jen smiled to herself thinking of Fliss's comments about his hands. Fliss was right, he did have lovely hands, they were large and strong, they could only be the hands of a man.

Suddenly it seemed a little awkward for them both to be squatting silently on the step in the rain and they quickly stood up.

'Okay, I have got to go' and was gone.

Mrs Pendlehurst was delighted with the gift

'He is like an artist' she said

The next day when Jen arrived home from taking Muffin for his walk, she was amazed to find an identical pot outside the door of her cottage, she was so pleased with it and kept looking out of the kitchen window when she passed. What should she do, should she ring him or send a thank you card? That seemed a little formal. In the end she thought she was bound to see him soon when he started work at Millstone and could thank him then. Fliss was intrigued when she saw the pot and used every opportunity to tease her about her admirer.

Work on the garden was delayed. There did not seem to be a break from the rain all through January and February, the sky a constant palette of steel grey and black, the days dark and dismal, the nights cold and windy. The garden was a quagmire, the normal spring display of snow drops and crocuses were swamped in the murky, wet earth, the lawn looked like marsh land.

They were luckier than others in the village though, some homes and businesses had been flooded when the riverbank had eventually burst. The promise of spring seemed to be a distant dream and the gradual lengthening of the days were practically unnoticeable.

The weather suited her mood, the weeks passing slowly in monotonous gloom. She wished she could just sleep the days away, but it was difficult enough sleeping at night. Days highlighted only by the texts and telephone calls from Laura and the anticipation and preparations for her homecoming. It had been arranged that she would come back for a few days to celebrate her birthday. Jen was so excited, they had made plans for the whole weekend, including a shopping trip on the Saturday, a meal out with their friends in the evening and lunch with Helen and her family on the Sunday.

Jen met Laura at the train station on Friday evening and within ten minutes had whisked her from a cold, wet station to the cosy cottage with burning log fire and her favourite dinner cooking. Muffin seemed even more excited than Jen and ran around the cottage like a crazed puppy. Laura put her bags in her room then came into the kitchen where Jen was serving their food.

'Yum, that smells delicious Mum, my favourite'

"Good, I hoped it still was'

'Mum, I have something to tell you and I can't wait another moment'

She took hold of Jen's hand across the table to ensure she had her total attention.

'Mum, I have met someone. Someone who is gorgeous and clever and funny and amazing' she gushed, her eyes wide and bright 'He is just so wonderful, and I am so, so happy'

'Wow' said Jen 'When did all this happen? You haven't said anything'

'I have really liked him for a long time, but we just started seeing each other about a month ago so I wanted to wait until I was home so I could tell you all about him'

'What's his name,' asked Jen 'Is he on the same course as you?'

'His name is Fin and no, he's not on my course, I met him at the gallery, he's an artist, well not professionally yet, but he is just so talented, so brilliant. Look,' she took her mobile phone out of her pocket "This is him'

She passed her phone over the table to Jen who could just make out the face of a young man with tied back long hair and a lovely smile.

'Isn't he gorgeous Mum?'

'Yes, he has a lovely smile. I am so happy for you' Jen said squeezing Laura's hand, 'maybe you can bring him home sometime, so I can meet him.'

'Actually, I was just coming to that,' said Laura 'Would it be okay to bring him home for the Easter holidays? I would love you to meet him and I was planning on having a

couple of weeks at home anyway.'
'Oh, okay, of course' replied Jen, not sure whether to be
happy that Laura was so keen for her meet Fin, or
disappointed that she would not have her to herself.
'Oh Mum, you will love him, and he can't wait to meet you,
I've told him all about you.'
'Oh dear, and he still wants to come?'
'Well I haven't told him everything, obviously, it would be
too embarrassing, and he would just do a runner'
'Oh, okay I will try not to get blind drunk, walk around
naked or talk about the body buried under the patio that
weekend. I will save that for his second visit'
'He probably wouldn't even notice, he is very laid back'
'That's good, I am sure he is very nice.'
'Mum, what is it, what's the matter? I know you, something
is worrying you, don't you want to meet Fin?'
'Yes, of course I do, I can't wait to meet him, I guess it's
just all come a bit out of the blue.'
'I know, I can't believe it myself, I didn't think he had even
noticed me and then suddenly one day we started chatting
and we just clicked and that was it. We haven't really been
apart ever since'
'That's lovely, honestly, I'm so pleased for you, will he be
able to stay the whole two weeks?'
'Oh, I'm not sure, but I hope he will at least be able to
spend the Bank Holiday weekend with us. Please do not go
to a lot of bother, just let's carry on as we normally do, I
know he will just fit in with us perfectly.'
Jen took a sip of her wine and looking down at her food
asked as nonchalantly as she could.
'Where is he going to sleep?'
'Oh Mum,' laughed Laura 'In with me of course'
'Right, yes of course, I was just checking' her eyes still
focused on her dinner.
'And before you start worrying about that, we are being
careful, I've been to the doctor and everything has been
sorted out'

'Well, that's good, I'm glad you are being so sensible, but knowing you I wouldn't expect anything less.'

After dinner they snuggled on the sofa beside the fire and caught up with all their news, Laura regularly checking her mobile for messages from Fin. Katie had come home for the weekend to celebrate Laura's birthday, so the next morning the three of them visited Boughton, shopping and lunch.

Jen had given Laura money for her birthday, so she enjoyed the novelty of buying new clothes.

In the end she decided on some new boots, jacket, and a stunning blue off the shoulder dress. This was not her normal style at all; she normally had far more bohemian tastes, but she looked exquisite in the figure-hugging dress. When she stepped out of the dressing room, really for the very first time, Jen noticed she was a grown woman.

That evening the three of them went to The Plough in the village with Helen, Mike, Jonty and Fliss for a celebratory meal. This was the closest thing to family that Laura had ever known, although they all missed having Henry and Hugo with them too. Jen looked around the table, getting them all into view, laughing and chatting. She held the picture of them all in her mind, freeze framed so the moment could be captured.

Laura had worn the new blue dress, not really suitable for a wet February night, but she wanted an excuse to wear it.

'Wow' said Jonty 'look at you'

When Laura was younger she had a huge crush on Jonty, but of course to him she was just his little sisters' friend. She often told Jen that when she grew up, she was going to marry Jonty and be Katie's sister, in the way that children simplify life. Not for the first time Jen looked at them both that night and thought wouldn't that have been perfect.

They had just finished dinner and were considering more drinks when Fliss noticed David Brook sat the bar, in the lounge area of the pub.

'I'll go and order the next round' said Jen, 'I need to have a word with David anyway.'

'Do you need my help?' whispered Fliss teasingly 'Or will I be cramping your style?'

'When I manage to find my style, I will start worry about you cramping it'

David was sat on a bar stool, looking at his mobile phone.

'Hello David'

He looked up seemingly surprised that anyone would approach him and know his name.

'I don't know if you remember me' she asked hesitantly, 'Jen. I work for Mrs Pendlehurst'

For an awkward moment he did not respond at all, just sat looking at her.

'Yes, of course I know who you are'

'Oh good' she replied, relieved 'I just wanted to thank you for the plants, they were so lovely and lasted for ages, in fact they are only dying off now. I wanted to thank you before, and thought you would be starting work on the garden, but then you didn't of course because of the weather'

She realised she was waffling and stopped.

Another awkward moment while he kept looking at her before seeming to understand that he was expected to respond.

'I'm glad you liked them'

'Yes, they were lovely, thank you'

Although he was still not the most comfortable person to be around, Jen noticed that he at least kept eye contact now. In fact, he had gone the other way, staring into her eyes intently. He looked quite different out of his heavy-duty waterproofs. He was wearing jeans and a well-fitting pale blue shirt, which defined his muscular shoulders and strong arms, she noticed that he also smelled lovely.

'Would you like a drink?' he asked

'Er, thank you, but no, I am just about to get some in for my friends' she answered, pointing over to their table, where she now noticed they were all watching them.

'Oh, right of course' he said looking away from her for the first time and taking a sip of his beer.

'But please, please let *me* get you a drink, to thank you for the flowers.'

'No thanks, I'm fine'

She felt that she had hurt him in some way, but she could not think what she had done wrong.

'You are welcome to join us, Fliss is here as well'

He looked at her as if what she had just suggested was ridiculous.

'Join you? He looked over at their table, where to her embarrassment everyone was looking back at them.

'It's my daughter's birthday' she said almost apologetically, then instantly cross with herself for feeling that she needed to make excuses to him.

'Er, no thanks, I was just leaving'

'Okay. Well, I guess I will see you when the weather improves, and you start on the garden.'

'Yes, I expect so' he said slipping off the bar stool and putting on his jacket. 'Bye then'

Jen and Laura spent the next day at Upper Leys Farm while the girls were out with the horses, Jen helped Helen with the lunch. Mikes parents had died a few years ago so the farm was now run by Mike, Jonty and Helen.

The huge kitchen had an enormous old pine table and an ancient Aga sat in the inglenook fireplace with an assortment of dog beds in front of it. A Welsh dresser that had been Mike's grandmothers ran along one wall, crammed with dishes, plates, photographs, letters and pots brimming with odds and ends. The huge butler sink was in front of the window, looking out over the fields and distant hills.

The house had originally been built by Mike's great grandparents and there were still remnants of their lives in view today. On the wall above the Aga hung his great grandmothers copper pots; and a cut glass trifle dish of hers sat on the Welsh dresser. His grandfather's old oak writing desk still sat in the office, although it was now the home of the computer.

But it was the little everyday items still in use that always enchanted Jen. Opening the cutlery draw there were serving spoons that had been in use for over a hundred years. Helen still rolled out her pastry with a ceramic rolling pin that had been in the hands of all the women who had lived in the house.

The needles were kept in a little pin cushion that Mikes great grandmother had lovingly made and embroidered with little hearts and her initials. There was a tiny three legged stool that all the children through the generations had loved to use. They also had a family bible in the back of which they recorded all the births, marriages and deaths in the family going back to 1840.

Within these four walls the family could feel, touch and see their roots.

They had roots running deep into the pastures and up to the hills, they knew who they were, where they had come from, and where they were going. Whatever the world outside the farm gates threw at them, they could come in and know their place, know their people. It was solid and safe and just what Jen had always dreamed of.

Fliss arrived with bottles of bubbly to continue the weekend birthday celebrations. They sat down to a delicious roast leg of lamb that had been cooking slowly all morning then rhubarb crumble and lemon meringue for dessert. The day was as overcast as usual and it was already dark when Jen and Laura said their goodbyes and left for the station.

Laura hugged her mum tightly as they waited on the platform for the train.

'Soon it will be Easter and I will be back with Fin, I am so excited, I can't wait for you to meet him'

'I know Lolly, I can't wait either. Will he be there to meet you at the station when you get back to uni?'

'No, he is working today, he is doing some shifts in a cocktail bar at the moment, but he will come over as soon as he finishes'

'Oh, that's good' answered Jen, grateful that there was another person looking out for Laura, that someone else in the world was caring for her.

Before she could ask any more questions, the train arrived and again Laura was gone. It felt like déjà vu as she drove back through the village alone again, back to the dark empty cottage. When she parked her car, she saw beside the door a new, fresh, vibrant planted pot of spring bulbs, where the old, fading flowers had been.

She stopped and smiled, her mood instantly lifted, what a lovely way to brighten her sad and lonely return she thought. Unexpectedly she was gripped with an overwhelming feeling of disappointment at not being home when David had delivered them.

CHAPTER 7

Returning home from work the next day, Jen felt unable to settle, she pulled on her wellingtons, wrapped up against the rain and took Muffin for a long muddy walk along the river and through the woods, which normally did the trick. But walking back through her door, she still felt the same. The cottage, normally her sanctuary, felt like it was closing in on her, suffocating her.

She did not want to sit, didn't want to eat, she paced around the small sitting room full of restless energy. For the first time in years she felt she wanted to break free of this life, wanted to tear down the four walls and leave behind everything she was and everything she had. Surprisingly, it now didn't seem to be enough, she wanted more.

The darkness was all around her, worse than it had been for a while, but whereas she normally felt more in control of her anxiety in the safety of her home, she felt compelled to run away from it, to escape and leave it festering behind her.

She looked out of the kitchen window at the terracotta pot of bright little flowers sat in their moss bed. She had noticed when walking Muffin down the driveway earlier, that David had not replaced Mrs Pendlehurst's plants, only hers. He had come here just for her. He liked her, he may not have said anything, but there was something about the way he looked at her.

Suddenly she desperately needed to speak to him, to see him. She Googled the website of his nursery finding the telephone number and started to call. Then stopped the call before the dialing tone had begun.

'What am I doing?'

Her heart was pounding; she put the mobile on the table and filled the kettle. What was she going to say? *'Thank you for my plants?'* What if he didn't say anything? Knowing him it would probably be awkward. What if he was busy or dismissive of her?

'Who did you say you are? No, I must have put them in the wrong place, they were meant for Mrs Pendlehurst, why would I give them to you?'

She made a cup of tea and sat down at the table playing out the possible scenarios of their conversation in her head.

'Hello, is that David, this is Jen, thank you for the lovely plants' No.

'Hello, this is Jen from Millstone House, thank you, the plant pot is lovely' No.

'Hello David, how kind of you to replace the flowers, may I buy you that drink sometime' No. No. No.

'David its Jen here, I'm so sad and so lonely, would you please come straight over?' Honest, but oh my god no. This was ridiculous, she didn't even know him, he could be married with a family, had her sad, lonely life got this desperate? She walked away and began pacing again, went back into the kitchen picked it up, put it back on the table, walked out of the kitchen and up the stairs absently into Laura's bedroom, standing in the doorway she looked around the room, her books, her photographs, her old teddy.

'For goodness sake' she hissed at herself and stomped determinedly down the stairs back to the kitchen and the mobile. She took a deep breath and rang the number carefully.

'Hello' said David's voice *'This is Meadow Farm Nursery, I am unavailable to take your call at the moment, please leave a message'*

She finished the call, all at once both relieved and disappointed.

Should she leave a message? Yes. She called the number again and listened to David's recorded response one more time whilst preparing her speech. The beep came, she opened her mouth but nothing came out. She ended the call again. Maybe I should just go and see him?

She decided she needed to find him. This was crazy, the rush of adrenaline made her laugh out loud. She rushed upstairs to change her clothes. Her wardrobe was full of practical, casual clothing, and while she wanted to look casual, she didn't want to look drab and frumpy. She put on her best jeans and a white vest; okay so far, but now what? A sensible jumper, a cosy fleece?

In desperation she went into Laura's bedroom and opened her wardrobe. The clothes were certainly brighter in here, but were they too young looking for her? A simple purple and white floral shirt caught her eye. She tried it on, tucking it into the jeans and looked in the mirror. Not too bad, she had long black boots that would look okay, but what about a jacket? Her only decent one was simple and practical and, she now decided, dull, dull, dull.

'Why don't I have any decent clothes?' she said to herself. 'Because you don't go anywhere to need them' she answered.

Jen had an idea to call Fliss; she would have jackets to suit all occasions, but what excuse could she give? She would be suspicious, she was like a hound dog and would never let a subject drop until she had the answers to her questions.

When they had first met, Fliss had made it her mission to 'find someone' for Jen, even though Jen constantly made it clear that she was not interested. There had been some excruciating moments when a 'surprise' guest would turn up at one of Fliss's gatherings. Jen would plead with her not to do it again.

'Do what?' would ask Fliss innocently, 'I didn't even know he was coming, but since he is here, what do you think of him?'

Or she would inform Jen about any single men moving into the village, pointing them out in the pub and seeing if she may be interested to meet them. Or make it her business to discover details about any single fathers of the children at the local school. Her children did not even attend that school, so goodness knows where her information was coming from. There was no stopping her, and it was never subtle. She simply didn't believe that Jen could possibly be happy without a man in her life.

But since her own marriage breakup she had thankfully given up on this task. Maybe she now thought that having a man in your life did not guarantee happiness, or maybe she was now focusing her energy into finding someone for herself.

Whichever way it was, it was a relief, and Jen certainly did not want to give her any encouragement to start looking again. No, she would have to just wear her own jacket and be sure to go clothes shopping soon.

She sat down on Laura's bed and opened her bedside cabinet laying her make up collection out on the top, there was far more to choose from here, even though they were the remnants she had left behind, than in her own paltry make-up bag which contained a mascara, face powder and a tube of lip salve.

Jen laid out the array of different sized brushes, she had no idea what their purpose was, but choosing one she applied a foundation creme and with another a translucent powder. She chose a smoky grey eye shadow and started sweeping yet another brush over her eyelids. She stared at herself in the mirror.

'What the hell are you doing? This is madness.' She started giggling. She could not remember a time for many years that she had felt driven to act so spontaneously, but for the first time in a while she felt alive. Today she needed more than her safe routine.

She applied mascara and eye liner and brushed her hair, should she pin it up? She normally just wore it in a ponytail but maybe she could use some of Laura's clips?

'When did I last visit the hairdresser, not for years?'

She decided to just leave it loose and finding a lip gloss palette added a soft red pout. She sat there staring at herself in the mirror, turning her face from side to side. She could not remember the last time she had worn so much make up, probably when she was at college. She looked completely different, felt completely different. She wasn't just a mum or housekeeper, she looked like a woman. Maybe Fliss had been right all along and she did need a man in her life.

She had closed down that part of herself, unconsciously choosing not to have a man in their lives, not to risk anyone getting too close, discovering too much. Men could be dangerous; they could hurt them.

But maybe those pheromones that Fliss talked about had been awakened from their hibernation. Possibly David had noticed something more in her, but there again she may just be acting like an idiot.

Fifteen minutes later she was driving along the wooded lane just outside the village of Bellwick. Her heart was racing, her palms clammy on the steering wheel, she noticed up ahead the sign and entrance of Meadow Farm Nursery. She kept on driving past the entrance until she reached a parking and picnic area in the woods which she pulled into. She remembered she used to bring Laura here for walks when she was little, and now here she was stalking a man who had given her a plant pot! She wanted to giggle again.

Jen turned the car around and drove slowly back to the nursery. When she reached the sign and entrance again, she indicated, pulled into a small slip road and stopped in front of electric gates. On a metal post next to the gate she noticed an intercom system. She sat in the car for a moment, not sure what to do, she was not expecting this. Why could it have not been a normal plant nursery, or some sort of garden centre, open to the public, she had her plan ready for that, played over and over on the drive there.

She would be browsing the rows of plants, seemingly interested in some new bedding for her tiny garden. David would be working in a large greenhouse, he would look up and notice her and come over. She even had their conversation worked out in her head, her surprise at seeing him, his delight at seeing her, he asking her if she had time for a coffee, or lunch or perhaps dinner.

Now that was not going happen. Now she was stuck behind these metal gates with no excuse to go through them.

Jen almost decided to just leave and go home, but she knew that if she did, she would regret it. She walked over to the intercom system and studied it for a while. There was a black button to push and an area to talk into. Jen held her breath and pushed the button.

'Hello, may I help you?'

It was a woman's voice. For some reason Jen had not expected that. The woman sounded young, was it his daughter or young wife or partner, maybe she should just leave.

'Hello, may I help you?'

Jen was frozen to the spot, staring at the intercom.

'Hello. Hello, may I help you?'

'Hello, can you hear me?'

Jen took a deep breath 'Hello, is David Brook there please?'

'No, he's not I am afraid, may I help you?'

'Ah, don't worry' stuttered Jen slightly 'It doesn't matter, I need to talk to him really'

'Oh, what about? Are you sure I can't help you?'

Did Jen hear suspicion in this woman's voice?

'Uh, Mr Brook is doing some work at Millstone House, Long Bridge, we were just wondering if he had any date in mind for starting yet'

'Oh right, okay' Was that relief in the woman's voice? 'I am afraid that David is away for a few weeks working in Italy, shall I get him to call you when he is back, Mrs Pendlehurst?'

She even knows the name, thought Jen, she must know everything about him. They must discuss Millstone, Mrs Pendlehurst, her?

'Or would you prefer me to ask him to ring you, I will be talking to him later this evening' the voice went on.

This evening, so she is obviously not just staff, not just working there during the day, she is going to be there this evening, waiting for his call.

'No, don't worry, there is no rush, I will talk to him when he gets back'

'Okay, thank you Mrs Pendlehurst, goodbye'

'Bye'

She stood there staring at the intercom for a while thinking about the conversation. She felt deflated, is he married? Surely Fliss would have had that information knowing her.

'Sod it' she got back in her car, turned it around and headed towards Boughton deciding to spend the rest of the day clothes shopping.

CHAPTER 8

Another three weeks passed before at last there were some signs of spring. Daylight and birdsong now started the mornings and on brighter days you could even feel the frail warmth of the sun.

Jen had been keeping herself busy, maybe a little manically so. She had thoroughly spring cleaned every room in the cottage, repainted the sitting room, kitchen, and bathroom, cleaned the windows, tidied the small garden, planned the meals for Laura's return and stocked the larder and fridge. There had also been extra hours to work at Millstone as Mrs Pendlehurst's nephew from Canada was coming to England for the summer to research his latest book and would be based at the house for most of that time. Jen had prepared the best guest room for his stay and had aired and cleaned the other rooms of the house that were now not used.

Mrs Pendlehurst was extremely excited at having her nephew stay with her, she had not seen him for sixteen years, but had always been interested in his career as a journalist and more recently an author. She had filled vases with cut spring flowers from the garden and placed them around the house, and had persuaded him to give a talk about his work and travels to the local Women's Institute while he was staying, proud to be able to show him off to the other ladies.

Jen felt so much better being busy, she enjoyed waking early with a list of jobs she needed to achieve that day, mentally ticking each of them off. That was her problem she had decided, far too much time on her hands, too much time to indulge herself with too many thoughts. Too much time to very nearly make a fool of herself chasing some stranger because she was lonely and sad.

She felt embarrassed every time she thought about the visit to the nursery, what on earth was going through her head? It was just not like her to act so impulsively and was now so relieved that David had not been there that day, it was a lucky escape and thank goodness no one needed to know how silly she had been.

Once Easter was over, she was determined to find something more to occupy her time, maybe find some voluntary work, or possibly take a course in something, maybe both. It felt so much better to go to bed tired and be able to sleep deeply throughout the night.

She felt strangely nervous about the Easter Holidays. She wanted to welcome Fin to their home, but apart from sleepovers with friends when she was younger, there had never been anyone staying with them for any length of time, certainly not a boy.

Laura had a few boyfriends at school, but nothing serious. She had asked Jen not to make any fuss and for them to just continue as they would normally. But Jen could not imagine the two them sat around in their pyjamas all evening watching girlie films and stuffing themselves with chocolate easter eggs.

On the Thursday morning Jen awoke to bird song and a cloudless blue sky, Laura and Fin were coming home today. She took time wondering what to wear, she did not want to let Laura down and dress too casually but also didn't want to look like she had made too much of an effort. Eventually she decided on wearing jeans but with her new blouse and jacket, she walked to the village bakery to buy Laura's favourite rye loaf, and a white farmhouse just in case Fin would prefer that.

Walking back to the cottage, her heart jumped to see David's Land Rover parked outside. He was sat in the driver seat, window open, arm resting on the sill, beside him his black Labrador.

'Oh hello, are you looking for Mrs Pendlehurst?' She is probably at a church meeting, but I can leave her a message'

The Labrador stretched across David's knee putting his head out of the window with his best impression of a smile, tail wagging.

David didn't reply, just stroked the dogs' head.

Why was she suddenly angry with him? He had simply given her a pot of flowers and then got on with his life, this was ridiculous, but she could not stop herself, possibly it was his silence and smug smile.

'Look, I'm sorry' she continued 'I am rather busy at the moment, I'm just going out, is there any message you want me to give her'

'Why did you come to the nursery?' he asked still stroking the dogs' ear.

'I, I didn't' She said flushed, 'Well, I did, but I just needed to know when you were planning on starting work on the garden'

'Why?' he looked up at her.

'Because I....' she looked at the ground for inspiration

'Okay, I just thought it would be rude not to thank you for the flowers, as I was passing that way anyway because I was on my way to Boughton. I was out clothes shopping for the day and happened to pass your place'

Oh, shut up! She thought to herself, stop waffling, but could not stop herself.

'When I was going along the Boughton Road I noticed the Meadow View Nursery sign and simply pulled over to thank you'

She looked up to see him smiling at her.

He had a lovely smile she noticed. Was he laughing at her?
'Did you buy that jacket?'
'What?'
'When you drove past my place on your way to go
shopping, did you buy that jacket?'
'Yes, I did actually'
'It's very nice, the colour suits you'
Was he being sarcastic?
'Thank you'
'You're welcome. It's just a shame I was not at home when
you called, isn't it'
'Well....never mind, I have thanked you now'
'Yep'
They were both silent for a moment.
'Well, I will let you get on, I don't want to hold you up as
you are busy and just about to go out'
'Okay bye'
He reversed the vehicle and left.
An hour later she was and sat on a bench, waiting for the
train. She was early but felt the need to get out of the
house and it was lovely being able to enjoy the sunshine,
eventually the train pulled into the station.
As it came to a stop Laura swung open a door and stepped
onto the platform, she immediately spotted Jen and waved
excitedly. Fin stepped down from the train behind her
carrying her heavy bag. She ran over and hugged Jen
tightly.
'Mum' she said, stepping aside 'this is Fin, Fin this is my
Mum, Jen'
'Hello Fin, lovely to meet you'
Fin kissed Jen on the cheek.
'Hi Jen' he said, 'Great to meet you too at last. You two
look so alike, you are just a taller version of Laura'
'Only by a little bit and I might still be growing' laughed
Laura
'Come on' she said, taking him by the hand 'I have so
much I want to show you'

As they walked towards the car park, Jen felt slightly dazed. She was not sure what she had been expecting, but even with his boyish good looks, long hair and endearing crooked smile Fin was far older than she had anticipated. He must be at least 30 probably older, it was hard to tell.

CHAPTER 9

All through lunch it was difficult for Jen not to keep staring at Fin, did he maybe just look older? She wanted to bombard him with questions but knew she could do nothing but be the perfect hostess or Laura would immediately pick up on it.

And what if she did ask him how old he was and he said 30, or even older, what could her response be that did not sound rude and overly protective. Lolly had only just turned nineteen, okay not a child, but somehow not an adult either.

He was charming company, his easy boyish smile, shoulder length dark blond hair, jewellery and clothes made him look more like a surfer than an artist, and the slight accent emphasised this even more, Australian maybe she thought. After lunch Fin and Laura took Muffin for a walk in Trinket Wood.

As soon as they left the house Jen rang Fliss.

'Well,' asked Fliss immediately 'What's he like?'

'He's old'

'What do you mean old, 50s, 60s, 70s?'

'No not that old, but definitely 30s, I think'

'30s is not old. If he is an artist, he is probably a bohemian type and young at heart'

'Laura is just 19, she may have the head of a 30 year old, but she definitely has the heart of a 19 year old and the experience of a 19 year old. When you meet him later tonight, I want you to ask him all the questions that I can't'.

'Like what?'

'How old he is, is he married, has he any children, how does he earn a living, is he a drug addict or alcoholic, what are his plans for the future, does he wear condoms, you know the sort of thing.'

'Oh, my goodness, how long have I got? Should I bring some rope to tie him to a chair and a cattle prod so that I can interrogate him properly'

'If that is what it takes then yes'

'Are you maybe being a little over protective, or paranoid?'

'Just do it, I am relying on you. Poking your nose into other people's lives is your specialty. We will see you at 7.30, make sure you are sitting next to him, love you, bye'

They had booked a table at The Plough that evening to celebrate the girls being home and for them all to meet Fin. Hopefully the rest of the group would be able to see why she was concerned and maybe give her some advice. But Fliss was the best one to extract any information, and that would definitely not make Laura suspicious, Fliss interrogated everyone she met.

Katie was home and Jonty was bringing his new girlfriend Milly. Just Hugo and Henry were still missing from the group, but Fliss was already planning their homecoming in a couple of months. When they arrived Fliss made sure to sit next to Fin as instructed and Jen was pleased to see them talking, the interrogation seemingly going well.

Jen loved the evening, but felt distracted, she couldn't stop herself turning to look at the door every time someone arrived, a little disappointed each time it was not David.

At last, towards the end of the evening, there was the opportunity to follow Fliss into the ladies' cloak room.

'Well,' Jen whispered 'What did you think of him?'

'Oh he is lovely'

'Yes, but what did you find out about him?'

'Um, he went to art school, he has travelled a lot and spent a number of years in Australia, his mother died when he was fifteen, he has an older brother called Jake and they grew up in Guildford.'

'Is that it? You were talking for ages'

Fliss looked at her uneasily and continued quickly 'Okay, he is 35 and has a four year old son who lives with his mother in Australia'

'He's 35! What! He is old enough to be ......'

The door opened to a suspiciously silent room. Thank goodness it was Helen.

'What is going on you two? You have both been acting weird all night. Fliss you have been hogging poor Fin all evening, he looks exhausted. And Jen, you have been staring at Fliss and Fin and then jumping every time the door opened. What are you both up to?'

'Helen' whispered Jen theatrically 'I have just found out that Fin is 35 years old, that's too old for Laura isn't it? Imagine if it was Katie who had brought him home, what would you think?'

'Well, I have not had a chance to talk to him because he couldn't get away from Fliss for two minutes, but he seems nice enough, yes maybe he is a little too old for Laura. But listen to me, if Laura is fond of him, the only thing you can do is support and trust her judgement. If she feels in any way that you are against him, she will naturally take his side. She is young and in love, it's only natural that she will act that way. She must feel that you are on her side whatever her choices, then if anything goes wrong, she will know she can talk to you.

Anyway, who knows, this may be the real thing, she just may have met the real love of her life at a young age, and they stay together. I met Mike when I was seventeen'

'But he was nineteen, that's different'

'Sometimes I am so glad I had two boys' interrupted Fliss

'But what can I do? I can't just sit by and watch her get hurt'

'Yes, you can, its all you can do if you don't want to push her away' said Helen, 'you must remember what first love is like?'

'No, I don't think I do, I have never loved anyone'

'Never?' asked Fliss 'Not even your first crush, your first boyfriend, not Laura's father?'

'No. Nobody'

'Well trust me then' said Helen 'You really must let her go and make her own mistakes, even if it is painful to watch'

'Otherwise you will be like my mother when I met James, she despised him and begged me not to marry him, we had so many arguments about him, she pleaded with me but I still married him. I wish I had listened to her now'

'That is very reassuring Fliss, thanks for that!'

'Go back out there' said Helen 'Enjoy the evening and just look how happy Laura is, don't spoil everything for her or for you, or believe me she will not even bother to bring her next boyfriend home if you carry on acting like this'

Fin stayed for four days, four days of sunshine, so the two of them were out for most of that time. When they were at home Jen really did her best to take heed of Helen's advice, and try not to judge Fin, nor question Laura.

Of course, she knew, as always, that Helen was right, she always had a calm balanced view of situations. At times it was still difficult, but instead of worrying and finding fault, she tried her best to just concentrate on seeing Laura so happy.

On his last evening, Fin sat on the sofa with Jen while Laura was having a bath.

'Thanks so much for having me stay Jen, you have been great'

'Not at all, it has been lovely to meet you'

'That is very kind and polite of you, but I am sure it has not been easy. Look, I know Laura didn't tell you how old I am, I did ask her to tell you before I arrived but she was

worried that you would freak out and pre judge me.'
'Not at all Fin, it's not my business who………..'
'You don't have to lie, I know you were really uneasy when
I arrived, I could see the shock in your eyes when you
came and picked us up, and then you set Fliss the
Rottweiler on me' he laughed 'Laura told me you would do
that, and what to expect, she knows you too well'
Jen blushed, 'I am so sorry, it's just that she is my little girl
Fin, my whole world, and I love her so dearly, I can't help
but worry about her'
'I totally understand that, and that is something we have in
common, I am really fond of her too, and appreciate what
a great person she is. That is one good thing about your
daughter seeing an old man, I am not just some stupid kid
who does not know how to treat a girl, and I can also
appreciate that it must be hard when your daughter is
seeing someone who is not much younger than yourself'
'I am honestly happy that she is happy, really I am. Just
please don't hurt her, I know I am biased, but she is such
wonderful person'
'Listen, if anyone is going to get hurt it will probably be
me, I am sure she is going to get bored with this old fart
soon and want find some young stag before too long, but I
want you to know that I am looking out for her while she
is away from home.
 I too think she is great, you know, and I don't think you
are being biased at all, she is a wonderful girl'
He leaned over and patted her knee 'Right shall I go and
put the kettle on and makes us some tea?'
The next morning, they dropped Fin off at the station,
Laura had another week at home. Fin hugged Jen tightly as
he left, and thanked her again, much to Laura's obvious
pleasure, Jen hugged him back.
A week later and Jen was also taking Laura to the station.
As she drove back home, she suddenly realised that she did
not feel as distraught as the previous times, the anxiety and
worry were not nearly as bad as before. Was she getting

used to this new life maybe? Everybody had said it would get easier. Or maybe it was the reassurance of knowing that Fin was also looking out for Laura. Whatever the reason, for the first time in a long while she felt surprisingly calm and contented. She would take Muffin out for his walk, strip the beds, get the cottage back in order and then go and have a coffee with Helen, and thank her for her advice.

CHAPTER 10

The next day was busy, Edward Pendlehurst was arriving at Millstone that evening after spending his first few days in England visiting a friend in London. Jen wanted everything to be perfect at Millstone. It had been a number of years since anyone had stayed with Mrs Pendlehurst so she spent time airing and thoroughly cleaning his bedroom and the guest bathroom.

When she was happy that all was perfect in the house she then went shopping and returned to cook a beef casserole, dauphinoise potatoes and a lemon meringue, using the best china, cutlery and linen to lay the mahogany dining table ready for their dinner.

She loved this house and was so pleased to see it back to its full glory, back to how it should be. It had felt cold and sad with so many of the rooms unused for such a long time, now it seemed to have come back to life. It was a house built for people to use, a house for families. As the sun shone through its elegant long windows and reflected on the wood and brass, it was once again looking at its elegant best, it smelt of wax polish and spring flowers.

At 6.30 that evening she was curled up on the sofa in her pyjama's and dressing gown after taking Muffin for a walk and having a bath, when she heard a vehicle on the gravel drive. She decided it must be Edward arriving, so she was surprised to hear a knock at her door. Pulling her dressing gown around herself tightly she opened it slightly.

'Ah, your home' said David 'I called around earlier, but you were out'

'Did you? I was probably walking Muffin'

Oh, my goodness, what was he doing here. She kept the door slightly open and tried to step back into the shadows, she looked a mess! Her hair was still damp and unbrushed, and there was sure to be smudged mascara around her eyes, and to top it all she had on her scruffiest dressing gown and old slippers that had been slightly chewed by Muffin.

'Is something wrong?' he asked

'No. I am just not dressed for visitors'

'Should I have called first and made an appointment?' he smiled

'Well, yes'

'Do you want me to leave?'

'Well… I don't know....That's up to you'

He gently pushed the door open wider and slowly looked her up and down smiling.

'You are right, you were not expecting visitors'

She tried to rub the mascara from under her eyes and pull her fingers through her hair.

'I have just had a bath'

'Yes, I can see that'

He stepped closer and brushed away a tangle of hair that was clinging to her face

'You smell lovely' he said breathing in her hair 'Even if you look like a panda'

Jen stepped back.

'Why are you here?' she asked more abruptly than she intended.

'I thought I had better keep you up to date with my diary as you are so interested'

Was he mocking her? He was smiling and had obviously gone out of his way to see her, but was he just playing with her? She did not know how these games worked. He could be married, the female voice over the intercom, perhaps? It was so hard to read him, he seemed to be grumpy one minute and the next flirtatious.

'I just wanted to let you know that I am back in Italy next week but will start the work here in two weeks'

'Okay, I will let Mrs Pendlehurst know'

'She already knows. I just thought that you may be interested'

'It's nothing to do with me when you start work here or where you are going, you didn't need to come and tell me. Anyway, it's getting a bit chilly stood here, I had better go'

The cocky smile disappeared, and he looked upset. He was infuriating.

'Are you not going to invite me in?'

'No, I am not dressed, and as you kindly pointed out I am not prepared for visitors, and apparently look like a panda. To be honest I have no idea what you want, you just keep turning up unexpectedly and uninvited to mock me'

'I am not mocking you, I just wanted to see you'

'But you just turn up out of the blue, I don't like it'

'Okay'

He turned to walk away but then stopped and turned back to face her.

'This is really pissing me off, we are not kids. It's not just what I want from you, what do you want from me, you are sending mixed messages'

'I honestly don't really know'

'Okay, shall I make an appointment next time? Are you free a week on Saturday?

'Um, I might be'

He walked back over to her

'Whats your number'

He stepped just inside the door and handed her his mobile to put her number in. It felt strange to have him inside her home, have him stood so close to her.

'Okay I will call you. I guess I had better be going then'

'Yes, I guess'

He leaned down and kissed her cheek gently.

'I guess I had better be going'

'I guess' said Jen quietly

Gently taking the belt of her dressing gown he pulled her towards him and kissed her lips looking into her eyes.

'By the way, I didn't want to say anything before, but I am rather keen on pandas'

He kissed her mouth softly again, slipping his arms around her waist.

'Maybe you should wear some proper clothes though next time if we are going out' kissing her again.

'Unless you have changed your mind about me coming in' he opened her dressing gown and leaned back to look her up and down' Because I am also fond of pink fleecy pyjamas'

David pulled her dressing gown back around her and tied the belt again, pulling her closer with it and kissed her again.

Jen was literally breathless, her heart pounding. The feel of his touch, his arms around her, his hands on her back, his body pressed so closely and the way he looked at her, made her forget to breathe.

Something stirred deep inside, her whole body yielding to his touch. He could sense her softening into his arms, moulding into him, and he leaned down to kiss her neck. She heard a soft noise come from deep inside her.

They heard a car on the gravel drive, this would be Edward. His spell was broken. She moved slightly away from him and pulled her dressing gown tightly around herself again.

'You really are into pandas in fleecy pyjamas, aren't you'

'I don't care what you wear' he said, brushing her hair from her face 'Let's just stop all the games though can we?'

'I didn't know I was playing any'

'Yes, you did'

'I didn't know you even knew who I was'

'I have seen you about'

'Oh really'

'You used to walk your dog past the Robinsons garden every day when we were working there, he would jump up to wall and play with Pippa, my dog. I started looking forward to seeing you'

'You did?'

'Yes, your walk, your smile, your laugh, I used to make excuses to be there'

'I remember seeing you, but I don't remember you ever talking to me or anything'

'No. I said hello to you once, but you were more interested in the dogs. Anyway, I wouldn't have said anything with the men working there'

'Oh really? I'm sorry, I don't remember that at all'

'I also saw you in the pub a few times with your friends'

'You never spoke to me there either.'

'It was difficult, and you were always with that scary one'

'Ha, you mean Fliss, she is not scary. Well maybe a little bit until you get to know her'

'The time was never right'

'No, the time was not right for me either'

He kissed her mouth gently again

'Anyway, once you had started stalking me I knew that I had better make a move before you embarrass yourself'

'Stalking you, what do you mean?' laughed Jen

'When Lizzy told me Mrs Pendlehurst had called around to see me I was surprised. When she described what she looked like and the fact that she had hung around staring at the camera and not talking I had to have a look at the film, and there you were'

'There was a camera? Oh no don't say that! said Jen covering her face with embarrassment.

'Yep, I have kept the tape as evidence just in case there is ever a police case against you'

'Oh no don't, how embarrassing, a camera, oh no'
He kissed her again
'It made my day seeing you come looking for me. Are you sure you don't want me to stay?'
'This is all so quick, too quick, it is just madness'
'You are right, I hoped to get to know you and take things slowly, well that was the plan before you started seducing me as soon as I walked in!'
She laughed and playfully punched him "I did not'
'Anyway, I am sure I can wait a few more weeks, it will give me something to look forward to coming back for'
'Um, by the way, Lizzy, is she............'
'Lizzy, is my niece and my assistant she lives in the apartment at my place.'
'Oh okay, I just wanted to be sure everything was above board'
He smiled at her 'Acute jealously. Another trait to add to my file on you'
'You know, you look so different when you are happy, smiling suits you'
'Then just make me happy'
He kissed her mouth again.
'I will see you soon, lets hope you have found your hairbrush by then' he winked and left.
Jen watched him drive away then shut the door. She stood for a few moments taking everything in. Did that really just happen? Muffin came and stood looking at her sensing in the way that dogs do that something was different. His head turned on the side looking at her and trying to understand.
'Come on Muffy, let's go and ring Fliss'
Fliss, insisted on coming straight over with a bottle of wine and they curled up on the sofa and talked through the whole scenario frame by frame, getting more and more giggly. Jen could not get to sleep for hours that night, her head full of David, reliving each moment, his touch, his smell, the feel of him against her.

When she awoke there was a message from him, already at the airport.

'*Will be thinking about you panda., maybe next time I have to go to Italy, you could come too? You are welcome to pack those lovely, chewed slippers, but best leave the fleecy pyjama's at home? XX*'

CHAPTER 11

Later that morning Jen was loading the dishwasher at
Millstone, her head still swimming with the events of the
previous evening, when Edward Pendlehurst walked into
the kitchen.
'Hi Jen, how wonderful to see you again, it has been such a
long time, how are you?'
Edward walked over and kissed her cheek, slightly
awkwardly.
She had not seen him for over sixteen years. He and his
parents had visited England and stayed at Millstone for a
few weeks the summer before Charles Pendlehurst had
died.
Edward was a few years younger than Jen and she
remembered him as a tall, skinny, shy young man, so was
surprised when she saw him again. He had filled out, and it
suited him. He was now tall and muscular, with an easy
smile of perfect white teeth.
'I am fine thank you Edward, and how are you?'
'I'm great, but please call me Ted, I don't think there is
anyone still alive except Aunt Rosemary who calls me
Edward'

'Oh okay, yes, of course. Mrs Pendlehurst has been really looking forward to you coming'

'Yes, it's great to be here again'

'I doubt if anything looks very much different from when you were last here'

'No, not at all, its like stepping back in time. You don't look any different either Jen, but I am guessing little Laura has changed?'

'Oh yes, she is all grown up, in fact she started university last autumn. I don't think you would recognise her now'

'That's crazy to think she is that old, I remember sitting at this table with her building houses with her bricks'

'Yes, I had forgotten that she was really fond of you and followed you about everywhere. I remember she used to make you give her piggyback rides'

'Ha yes, she was such a cute little girl, always giggling'

Jen took her phone out of her jeans pocket and showed him a photograph of Laura. The latest one, in her new blue dress.

'Wow look at her, she is lovely, you are very alike, how old is she now?'

'She was nineteen in February, I don't know where the time went'

'Nineteen. No, it doesn't seem possible, hopefully I will get to see her while I am here'

'Yes, she will be back at the end of term'

'You must miss her Jen'

'The house is certainly quiet, its just me and the dog now'

'Aunt Rosemary was telling me you have a dog. I wanted to ask you, would you mind if I take him for a walk sometime? If I remember right there are some great places to walk around here, and it is much more fun with a dog'

'Yes of course, he would love that, just let me know when you want him'

'Great thanks'

'Can I get you any tea or coffee?'

'No thank you, but actually I do have another favour to

ask. Would you mind accompanying me to one of the pubs in the village sometime? I am going to be staying here for a few months and it would be great to meet some of the locals, and have somewhere to go and relax in the evenings, I hate the thought of just sitting in here on my own every evening when aunt Rosemary has gone to bed, I am not very good with my own company'

'Um yes, of course, is your new book set around here?'

'Not really, but it is so much easier to have a base to work from. When I told Aunt Rosemary I would be in England for a few months, she insisted that I stay here rather than rent somewhere, which was too kind an offer not to accept.'

'Yes, she is very proud of your work'

'Ah is she, that's nice. So, getting back to the pub. How about tomorrow night, we could have dinner, if you are free then'

'Uh sorry, I was planning on seeing a friend tomorrow night' Jen lied

'Well, could I take you both for dinner, if that's okay with you?'

'Um, I am sure that will be fine, thank you Edward.....Ted'

'Thats great, thanks Jen, I look forward to it, sorry to stop you working, I will let you get on. Really great to see you again, catch up with you tomorrow'

As soon as she arrived home she telephoned Fliss to persuade her to come the following evening.

'Oh my god' said Fliss 'Not another man after you, they are like buses, nothing for 20 years and then two of them in the same week, what are you suddenly doing right? If you carry on like this you will get a bad name for yourself'

'Ha, well you would know about that'

'Bitch! Well if I am helping you out you will at least have to share the surplus, I am not going to sit there while this one dribbles over you, feeling like a spare wheel'

'That is definitely not going happen, I think he is just worried about being lonely while he is staying in the village.

It is probably the choice of us taking him to the pub or Mrs Pendlehurst taking him to a church committee meeting'

'So you say. You were convinced that David was only interested in the garden. You just don't pick up on the signs, on body language, you are rubbish at knowing when someone is flirting with you'

'Well, he seemed more worried about being lonely than flirty but okay, I promise that if you will come tomorrow night, you can have Ted, poor chap, thrown into the lion's den. You will love him, he is handsome, tall, a dazzling smile and far too young for you. In fact, come to think of it, he is just your type'

'Okay, why didn't you just say that? What time?'

The following morning Jen was texting Laura when there was a quiet knock at the door.

'Hi Jen, sorry to disturb you, I was just planning on going for a walk and wondered if it would be okay to take Muffin with me, like you said?'

'Yes of course, come in, I will get his lead'

Muffin came running to the door at the sound of his lead being taken from its hook.

'Hello boy, my you're a handsome fella'

Muffin wagged his tail and circled Ted's legs in excitement, then sat on his feet and laid his head on his knee looking up with adoring soft brown eyes, he certainly knew all the tricks.

'Oh, you are gorgeous. Would you like to come with us too Jen? It's a beautiful morning'

Jen did not want to go. The last thing she wanted was to be forced to spend hours making polite conversation with someone she did not really know, and then have to do the same thing again this evening. Why couldn't he go by himself, or spend some time with his aunt, or just get on with his writing? But she saw the pleading look,. Muffin himself could learn a thing or two from this man.

'Okay, but I cannot be too long I'm afraid'

'No, no of course, we won't stay out too long'

They walked along the footpath of the field opposite, then over a sty into Trinket Woods, the bright new green canopy was just starting to open above them, and the sunshine dappled their path. Muffin ran ahead, discovering new smells and chasing squirrels.

Before long she had to admit, Ted was brilliant company. He had lived a very interesting life and was a natural story teller. He had spent years travelling to incredible places as a journalist and author and meeting fascinating people, he was very open about his life and loves too. She had hardly left this village in all that time.

He was also naturally funny, and immensely charming. He seemed genuinely interested to know all about her life, which was flattering, even though she was sure it was just out of politeness. He was extremely good at making you feel that you and your humdrum life were fascinating, which must be a superb tool for a journalist to use as an interviewing technique she guessed.

They had walked for over an hour and were nearly in the next village of Brampton, when they came to The Fox pub. 'Shall we stop here and have something to eat, or a coffee?' He asked

'I haven't brought any money with me, and Muffin is filthy.'

'That's no problem, we can sit out here in the garden, it should be warm if we find a sunny spot, and I have money on me. You choose a table, and I will pick up some menus. What would you like to drink?'

They both decided on the local real ale and a ploughman's lunch.

'What is your new book about?' asked Jen while they were eating

'It's a historical biography'

'So where is it set?'

'It's mainly based in Oxford so I will be there some of the time, following up my research'

'That will be interesting'
'Have you ever been there?'
'No, I haven't unfortunately'
'Then why don't you come to Oxford with me sometime? Would you do that?'
'Ha, I don't know, it depends when it is, if Laura is home or if I am working, or anything'
He reached over the wooden table and took her hand.
'Just tell me you will come with me to Oxford sometime, I am sure you will love it'
Those puppy dog eyes again.
'Okay, yes, I would like that, thank you'
They did not get home until midafternoon. It had been a lovely day, he was such easy company. There were not many men in Jen's life that she felt comfortable with, in fact apart from Mike, she realised there were none.
When he left her at her door, he kissed her on the cheek.
'That was great, I am going to do a couple of hours work and will come and pick you up at 7 o'clock, then we can go and do some more eating'
Jen soaked in the bath before getting ready. She was really looking forward to this evening and spending more time with Ted.

CHAPTER 12

Fliss was surprised when she arrived at The Plough, she thought she had been invited to assist Jen entertain a stranger, help with the flow of conversation. So she was amused when she walked in to see Jen and Ted sat closely together deep in conversation. As she walked up to them, she almost felt she were intruding.

'You must be Fliss' said Ted standing and kissing her on the cheek 'It's so lovely to meet you, I have heard a lot about you'

'All bad I hope'

'No actually, I have been with a huge fan of yours all day, sit down and I will get you a drink, what would you like?'

'Thank you, a gin and tonic with ice please'

Ted went to the bar and Fliss sat down in his seat

'Well you two have got really cosy very quickly, but you were absolutely right, he is really yummy'

'Um, I need to apologise for getting you here under false pretenses because you haven't got a chance I'm afraid'

'Why? What do you mean?'

'He simply wouldn't be interested, you are the wrong sex'

'Bollocks'

'Trust me, you will love him, I have never met anyone like him'

And Jen was right, Fliss quickly fell under his spell.

'What are your plans for the rest of the week' she asked
'I am here for a few days and then I am staying in London
for a week, I have some research to do there, and I also
have Patrick' he smiled
'Patrick, who is Patrick?' asked Fliss
'He is a lovely guy who I first met in Vancouver and hope
to get to know better while I am here'
'Where did you meet him, is he a writer too?'
'No, he is a doctor, I met him while he was working in
Canada last year. To be honest with you both, I have
wanted to write this book for a number of years, but the
time has never been right. But when Patrick moved back to
London, it was a great excuse to be able to follow him over
here without looking too desperate. I decided it was fate.
The book needed writing'
'How romantic' said Fliss 'I hope he knows how lucky he
is'
'Oh, believe me, I'm the lucky one'
'Well, I hope you have a great week and maybe we can all
do this again soon, or you could both come over to mine'
'That sounds perfect. I am so glad I have found you both, I
would have been a bit lost here on my own. I don't want to
neglect Aunt Rosemary, but she goes to bed at 9 o'clock,
and I hate my own company'
'I am afraid there is not a lot around here to entertain you,
it is certainly not Vancouver. Although the following
Saturday is the village Spring Ball. Why don't we all go to
that, you could bring Patrick' said Fliss
'That sounds great, and I would certainly love to go but
Patrick works crazy shifts, he has struggled to get any time
off next week when I am staying with him, I doubt he
would be able to take more time off the following
weekend. Plus, even if he could come and stay how do I
explain him to Aunt Rosemary? We have never had that
conversation.'
'Do you know, I honestly think Mrs P would be fine' said
Fliss 'We expect older people to be shocked, but they have

lived longer and experienced more, if anything they tend to worry less about things like that as they get older, they have probably seen it all'

'Well maybe, I hope so, but I don't think I want to ask her if Patrick can stay over quite yet'

'If he wants to come anytime, he could always stay at the cottage if that makes it easier, I have a spare bedroom' said Jen 'But I'm sorry, the Spring Ball is a great idea, but I am not sure if I am free that evening, I am meant to be seeing David, at least I think I am. But you two go ahead, you will enjoy it Ted'

'Well let's see what happens over the next week, I will get a couple of tickets and we can always get extras a few days before if it turns out you are not seeing David or if Patrick is able to come' suggested Fliss

Ted left for London a few days later and on the Saturday Fliss and Jen had a day shopping in Boughton. She had still not heard from David so Fliss had persuaded her to buy a ticket for the Spring Ball anyway. Jen was not exaggerating when she said that she did not have anything appropriate to wear on the evening and Fliss simply wanted something new.

The Spring Ball was one of the main social events of the year in the village. It was always held at Montfield Hall, a former residence of a local Lord, and now a hotel and popular wedding venue. Jen had never been to the Ball, having always been perfectly happy to babysit for the other children if Fliss or Helen had been attending in the past. She was looking forward to going this year with Fliss and Ted, especially as she had still not heard from David. She did not want to be sitting around on Saturday evening waiting for him, in case as she feared, he may not show up. In the back of her mind she questioned herself if she had fully understood what day David had suggested, maybe it was the following Saturday. Did she even have the right day, or would he still be in Italy then, or flying back late that evening? She did not feel comfortable contacting him to ask, it all sounded a bit too desperate.

In the end Fliss suggested to cover all options they also buy David a ticket and leave it for him to collect at the reception.

By Saturday evening there had still been no contact from him. Jen was now annoyed, disappointed and a little embarrassed. At seven o'clock Ted came to collect her, looking very handsome in his tuxedo, hired for the occasion.

'Wow' he said 'You look stunning, you really are very beautiful you know'

'Ha, thank you Ted, no one has ever said that before'

'Well they should have'

Jen twirled around in her flowing red dress, she had taken time to curl her hair, bought new makeup and matching red nail varnish. Earlier she had taken a photograph of herself and sent it to Laura to check that everything looked okay and Laura had Face Timed her straight back so that she could see her properly.

'Oh, my goodness Mum, you look incredible, you have gone from a cute little caterpillar into a gorgeous butterfly in a day. I hardly recognise you'

'I hardly recognise myself, I don't look ridiculous, though do I? Are you sure it is not a bit over the top, is the red lipstick okay? I don't want to look like a clown.'

'Not at all, it is all perfect, I am so proud of you, make sure you take some photographs later and send them to me'

'Okay my darling, I think I need a glass of wine now to settle my nerves, talk to you tomorrow'

After leaving Davids ticket at the reception desk and drinking a second glass of wine Jen decided to text him.

'Not sure if I was meant to be seeing you this evening? I have not heard anything from you. If you do want to meet up I am at the Spring Ball, Montfield Hall, I have left a ticket for you at the reception desk if you want it'

The Hall looked amazing, glittering lights, candles, beautifully laid tables and the food and company were wonderful, but there was no sign of David, she could not stop herself looking towards the entrance every five minutes or so. When the band started playing a man Jen recognised slightly came over to their table to ask Fliss to dance.

Jen remembered him now, Peter, he and Fliss had been seeing each other briefly a few years ago, but it had never been serious. She remembered that at the time Peter had travelled extensively for work and when he was home spent the majority of his time with his teenage children from a previous marriage, so it never came to anything. Although watching them dancing together now there was obviously some chemistry between them. After two dances they came back to the table and Peter sat down to join them.

The band then played a slow dance and Ted took Jen's hand

'Come on, we have to give that lovely dress a whirl' and then whispered 'And leave these lovebirds to it'

Jen put her arms around his neck as they danced.

'Patrick is a very lucky man you know, I hope he knows that'

'Thanks, I hope you get to meet him someday soon, although I am the lucky one. I am also very lucky to have you, I can't tell you how much it means to me that we get along so well'

'Ah, that's a lovely thing to say, yes its great having this time together, I have really enjoyed you being here'

As they turned on the dance floor Jen looked over Ted's shoulder and saw David stood by the main door watching them.

She waved to him, but he did not move, just kept watching her. When the music finished Ted sat down at their table and she made her way over to David.

'Hello stranger, you made it then'

He stood motionless and looked her up and down then nodded over to their table for four where Fliss, Peter and

Ted were all in deep conversation.

'That looks cosy'

'What? Don't be silly, someone has just sat there for a moment, the seat is yours, why do you think I bought you a ticket? Come on, let's go sit down, I will get you a drink'

David did not move.

'Who is the one you were dancing with?'

'That is Ted Pendlehurst'

'Really? You two have got very friendly, very quickly'

'Yes, we have, you will like him too when you meet him. Come and sit down' she pulled him arm gently.

'No thanks I don't want to meet him or come and sit down'

'Well, what do you want?'

'I want to leave. Are you coming with me?'

'No, I can't leave, the evening has just started and I can't abandon my friends, that would look so rude, especially now Peter is on the scene, poor Ted will be on his own"

'Poor Ted' said David

'Dont be so silly David, you are being ridiculous'

'I hope you all have a very nice evening together, bye'

He turned to leave, but Jen grabbed his arm and pulled him around.

'What the hell is wrong with you, I am the one who should be angry with you, just come and sit down'

'No, I am not dressed for this and I am certainly not in the mood. I have come straight from the airport to see you, only to get a text that you are here having a great time with your new friend. You obviously prefer to spend the evening with him'

She let go of his arm.

'Go on then. Go home and sulk, because yes you're absolutely right, I would rather spend the evening with Ted than with you, all you ever do is make me miserable and somehow feel guilty when I have done nothing wrong. Every time I see you there is something about me that you don't like, so why not just keep away from me now'

She turned and left him watching her for a moment striding purposefully back to the table and Ted.

At the end of the evening Peter insisted that he would share a taxi home with Fliss, even though they lived in opposite directions.

Jen was just getting into her pyjamas when her phone rang. David, she thought. But it was Ted.

'Aunt Rosemary has had a fall, it looks like she has been here all evening, I've called an ambulance, but would you come over?'

She quickly got dressed and rushed over to Millstone, the ambulance had just arrived and the paramedics were asking Mrs Pendlehurst some questions. Jen was shocked at how dreadful she looked, she had no movement in her left arm and left leg and was shaking uncontrollably. It was hard to recognise this normally perfectly poised woman, who now so suddenly looked frail and vulnerable. The fear in her eyes was heartbreaking to see.

Jen rushed around packing an overnight bag and they followed the ambulance in Ted's car. By the time they had found a parking space and made their way to A & E, Mrs Pendlehurst was already in a cubicle.

'Oh, you didn't need to come, I don't want to be a bother, I am sure I will be fine' she said shakily.

She certainly did not sound sure. Jen pulled the thin blanket up to her shoulders.

'Don't be silly, you are no bother at all, we want to be here with you. What happened, can you remember?' asked Ted

'It was all so silly, I had made a cup of tea and I put it down on the side table and then bent down to pick up my book and suddenly I just fell forward and I couldn't get off the floor, I couldn't stand up'

'What time was that?'

'Oh, about 8 o'clock, I tried to crawl over to the telephone, but I just couldn't move' the fear was back in her eyes.

Ted kissed her forehead gently. 'Listen aunt Rosemary,

don't you worry about anything, we shall have you running about again good as new before you know it'

'I was just so relieved that you were staying with me Edward, that you were coming home, otherwise I may have been on the floor until Jen came on Monday morning.'

'Well I am here now, and you are safe, I am sure that the doctors will be able to sort everything out and will take good care of you'

She smiled politely but did not look at all convinced.

When the doctor arrived and started asking questions it became clear that this was not her first fall. Jen thought back to when David had carried her into the kitchen. They had thought that she had slipped on the mud, but apparently, she was now telling the doctor that she had also fallen in the church and had blamed that fall on a loose flagstone.

Dr Preston explained that these previous episodes had probably been a series of small strokes leading to this one. They stayed in the cubicle all night until the tests and paperwork had been completed and a porter eventually came to take Mrs Pendlehurst to a ward. Ted and Jen then left the hospital arriving home exhausted, totally drained.

'My god what a night' said Ted as they got out of the car 'It is going to feel strange staying in that big old house on my own'

'You can stay in Laura's room if you like'

'Really? Yes, I would like that, thanks'

As exhausted as she was Jen could not sleep. She could not get the look of panic in Mrs Pendlehursts eyes out of her mind. Nor the look of hurt in David's. Fears of her future came back again to haunt her. If Mrs Pendlehurst died or could no longer live at Millstone what would happen to her and Laura, where would they go, where would they live, what other job could she do?

She always knew that this day would come, that their

future here at Millstone was only viable while Mrs Pendlehurst needed her. Laura had two more years at university, but this was still her home and she would be back during the holidays, where else could she find for them?

CHAPTER 13

By mid-morning they were both up, Jen made them
scrambled eggs on toast and tea while Ted telephoned the
hospital for an update.
'Thankfully, Aunt Rosemary had a comfortable night, she
slept quite well and has eaten some breakfast, apparently
we are allowed to visit from 3pm' he reported.
They found Mrs Pendlehurst's old navy leather address
book and discussed who they should notify of her
situation, deciding eventually to telephone the vicar and
two of her friends who were on various committees. Mrs
Pendlehursts sister Dorothea had recently had a hip
replacement so they contacted her daughter Caroline, who
was very sorry to hear about poor Aunt Rosemary but was
afraid she could not visit or offer any help as her own
mother needed her full time attention at the moment.
Ted put the phone down and sighed
'Old age is crap. The longer you live the fewer people there
are left in your life who care. Look at this book it has pages
and pages of neatly crossed out names, most of them no
doubt now dead, it's really sad to look through, and this
amazing house and the life they built here, it's just a shell
now. She has all this and yet nobody who really cares, I feel

so guilty that I have not visited sooner she must have been so lonely'

Jen squeezed his arm. 'Don't feel guilty, it is certainly not your fault, you don't even live in the same country.

Caroline is also her niece you know, in fact she is her own sister's daughter so genetically closer than you, but I have never even met her, and she lives a few hours away.

I know it's sad, it is hard to bear thinking about the future sometimes.

Look at us two, we are going to be in the same position before we know it. I know I have Laura, but I would never want her to feel guilty about having to visit me, or look after me when I get old, I couldn't bare that, and hopefully she will have a family and a full life of her own, she may even live abroad, who knows. Then I will be on my own too'

Ted pulled her towards him and hugged her 'We will look out for each other'

She felt comforted in his arms, even though they had only really known each other for a few weeks she felt incredibly close to him. But she also knew that in reality he would be going back to Canada in a few months and she would probably never see him again after that.

She looked up at him and smiled 'Oh if only you liked women'

'Ha, even if I did, how do you know you would be my type? I am sorry but you would be a bit on the skinny side for me. No, if I had the choice of you both I would have to choose Fliss' He laughed and squeezed her nose.

'We will be okay' he said 'We have a few years yet to find a family of our own'

'I'm not holding my breath. Only one man has really shown any interest in me for the last twenty years, and I cant be in the same place as him for 10 minutes without arguing. No, I will just stick to loving my dog, I am sure of being loved back there'

At three o'clock armed with books, magazines, reading glasses, fruit and her favourite liquorice they were sat around the hospital bed. Although still very grey looking Mrs Pendlehurst looked calmer and gave Jen instructions of who she needed to contact on the various committee meetings that she would miss.

'And don't forget that David Brook is starting work on the garden on Monday'

As if she had forgotten that.

On their way home they stopped at a pub for food, neither felt like cooking and as it turned out neither were particularly hungry.

They returned and walked Muffin through the fields, it was a beautiful evening, the first warm evening of the year, the smell of new life and warm earth filling their world.

'You must continue with your plans Ted, your research for the book and spending time with Patrick, that is what you are here for'

'No, it can wait, I can't leave you to deal with everything'

'Listen, if you were not here, I would be dealing with everything anyway, it's my job'

'I don't think this was in your contract' he smiled

'Contract? I don't remember ever having one'

'Yes you do, I have seen it'

'Really? Anyway I am not going to be needed at the house if there is nobody there so I have plenty of time to visit the hospital. I will let you know if I need you to come back for anything and will keep you updated every day'

'Well, we will see, I do have one request though, would you be okay with me staying with you at the cottage instead of Millstone, its far more homely at yours and I promise I will get out of your way during the day, I will work in Aunt Rosemary's study'

For a moment Jen did not answer. Her first thought was what if David saw him leaving in the mornings what would he think, but she could not say that.

'Yes of course, you are welcome to stay'

'Let me know when it is not fine though, when Laura is due back, or you are just fed up with me'

On Monday morning Jen went to Millstone as usual, she walked through the hallway and looked out of the porch window. There was David's vehicle along with another truck, but he must have been somewhere in the garden. She kept herself busy being careful not to disturb Ted in the study, then made them both lunch and he came through to the kitchen to join her. Jen was washing up their plates when the front doorbell rang.

'I'll go' said Ted

He returned after a few minutes.

'That was David, he was wanting to talk to Aunt Rosemary, my goodness he is certainly a broody soul. I got the distinct impression that I was the last person he was hoping to open the door. Gorgeous eyes though' he winked

'Oh, I am sorry, he is so rude and moody. I am sure it isn't just you though, he wouldn't have wanted to see me either'

'Anyway, I explained what has happened and asked him to continue as best he can, and we will convey any messages to Aunt Rosemary. He said he will not be personally working here, he is leaving his team to do the project, but I am to call him if there are any further instructions'

Ted saw the flash of disappointment in Jen's eyes.

'Why don't you just call him Jen and explain?'

'Explain what? That I waited two weeks for him to call me? Or that I kindly bought him a ticket to spend the evening with me? No, I have done nothing wrong, I am not chasing after him'

Ted held her shoulders gently.

'But you are cutting off your nose to spite your face. Maybe you should give him another chance, from what you have told me and what I have seen of him, David is obviously a guy who simply doesn't communicate too well, just like lots of other men, he gets frustrated and cross, but I don't think he is really bad.'

'You say that but who knows, I don't really know him at all. Is he worth taking the risk?'

'Sometimes you have to take a risk. Look at me coming to England chasing a man who I don't know has any true feelings for me. I am desperately clutching at straws trying to find a story to write about something I once overheard just as an excuse to be here. I am sure Patrick thinks I am stalking him'

'Meeting David was fun for a few weeks, it was exciting, but is it just because I was lonely? Maybe it would have been the same with anyone who happened to come along and give me some attention, that's not nearly enough to risk upsetting mine and Lolly's lives for'

'Yes you could be right, although Jen it is time to make a life for yourself and stop thinking of every situation from Laura's perspective, you know eventually, as you say, she will move on with her life and so must you'

'Yes, I know, you are right, but I honestly can't imagine any man being a part of my future, I can't see me ever settling down with anyone, I don't even understand the rules and games of it all'

For the rest of the week they followed a routine of Ted working in the study and then the two of them visiting the hospital together from 3pm to 6pm, then back to the cottage for supper cooked by Ted. On the Friday evening they went to the pub after the hospital and met with Helen, Mike, Fliss and the very attentive Peter.

They all chatted about lots of things, but subtly managed to skirt the question that Jen knew they must all be thinking, the white elephant in the room. What would she do if she is was no longer needed at Millstone House?

CHAPTER 14

The following morning Ted left for Oxford. Patrick was joining him for the weekend and then Ted was staying on in the city until Friday to continue his research. Jen had to persuade him not to cancel his plans and assure him that she was perfectly happy to visit the hospital every day. He eventually agreed to go on the promise that she would call him immediately if needed in any way. Whatever happened, she thought, he had to continue with his work, the book had already been commissioned and his time in England was passing so quickly.

As soon as he was gone Jen was surprised at just how much she missed him. Her days were again empty, walking Muffin in the morning, visiting the hospital in the afternoon and sitting alone in the evenings.

Since Laura had started university last autumn, she had gradually adapted to being on her own, but now after having Ted in her life and David in her thoughts, it seemed so much harder again.

Mrs Pendlehurst was stable and comfortable but the paralysis in her left-hand side was the same. Jen dreaded the daily hospital visits, it was much easier when Ted was there too, but on her own it was tough to know what to talk about, she found she was repeating the same questions every afternoon, occasionally though there were visitors from the church, which was a relief.

Jen telephoned Dorothea every few days with updates, she was of course recovering from a hip operation, but grateful for any news of her sister, and conveying messages from Dorothea gave Jen something to talk about. Both of their lives were in limbo, would Mrs Pendlehurst ever be able to come home, or would she need to move into a care home? Nothing was ever said, it felt as long as nobody mentioned the worst-case scenarios they would simply not happen, and their lives would merrily continue on as before.

On Friday morning Jen had a great idea. She would take photographs on her phone of the progress in the garden to show Mrs Pendlehurst when visiting the hospital that afternoon. Muffin came with her and they walked around to the front of the house, across the circle of driveway and through the huge wooden door of the walled garden.

Laura had loved to play in here when she was little.

She was not allowed near the vegetable plots, flower beds or greenhouse, but the rest of the three acres had consisted of a huge lawn with one end leading to the terrace and patio doors and the other to a copse of ancient oak and yew trees in front of the back wall. Laura used to say the wood was a fairy dell, but only she could see the fairies. When Jen opened the door and stepped into the garden, she questioned herself if she should in fact take any photographs at all.

The old greenhouse was gone, the vegetable plots, flower beds and some of the lawn had been dug up, leaving angry looking scars and large clumps of earth in her precious garden. The only sanctuary was the fairy wood, looking as tranquil and beautiful as always on this glorious bright morning, with its carpet of bluebells.

She walked over and wandered through the trees, listening to the bird song and enjoying the heady scent, even though it was still early in the day, it was already warm and the trees offered a canopy from the heat.

Muffin was busily running around chasing squirrels when he suddenly stopped, sniffed the air and ran full pelt back out onto the lawn. Jen watched to see him charging at David's black Labrador Pippa, who was now racing towards him. The two dogs stopped suddenly when they reached each other and performed the ritual sniffing before breaking off and chasing one another across the piles of earth.

Then she saw David walking through the gate carrying what she guessed were plans for the garden, he immediately noticed the dogs playing and looked towards the copse, but Jen was hidden in the shade. Two other men followed him through the gate, and David unrolled the plans on the patio table, the three men leaning over them. She would have liked to have stayed hidden and watched them from afar, but that was ridiculous, they could be working here all day, she could not suddenly appear from the copse in a couple of hours.

She decided to simply start taking the photographs as she had planned. That was the only excuse for being here, not that she needed an excuse. She tried to look as natural as possible while making an exaggerated point of taking several photographs of the garden from several different angles with her phone. As she got closer to the gate, she kept glancing towards the men but none of them seemed to have noticed her, or if they had they were ignoring her, even though the dogs were intent on their game, running around her legs and barking excitedly.

She climbed onto one of the mounds of earth to take a final photograph of the view looking back at the copse just as the dogs decided to race up the mound in front of her, knocking into her legs and throwing her off balance. She fell on her back and slid ungraciously down the soil to the bottom of the mound, jumping quickly to her feet she looked around, maybe nobody had noticed, but all three of the men were stood silently staring at her.

'Are you okay?' called over David

'Yes, I am fine thank you' she called back, brushing herself down 'Mrs Pendlehurst just wanted some photographs of the garden'

She held up her phone as evidence of her task.

'Was it a particularly good shot from down there?'

She glared at him

'Muffin, come on, come here, Muffin now'

She marched as proudly as she could out the garden door, her head held high. Muffin ran after her but so did Pippa.

'No Pippa, get back in'

She tried to hold the heavy door open whilst struggling to grab the Labradors collar. Pippa wriggled away from her grip and continued following Muffin across the driveway.

'Pippa, come here' she shouted angrily

The dog glanced back at her but completely ignored her. Suddenly David was at her side and whistled his dog, who spun around and came running back sitting dutifully at his feet with Muffin following behind.

Jen didn't know who she was angrier with, David, Pippa, or Muffin, who was now sat next to Pippa also looking up at David for further instructions.

'I don't know who is the more stubborn, you or your stupid dog' she said suddenly furious.

'Pippa isn't stubborn' he said calmly, stroking the dog behind her ears 'she simply likes people who are respectful and loyal'

'Oh, does she, well good for her'

'Yep, I can always trust Pippa'

'Well, maybe she hears from you when you go away for two weeks, instead of just ....'

She stopped realising how ridiculous her ranting sounded.

He looked down at her calmly. For a moment she thought he was going to kiss her, he looked at her lips and then back to her eyes slowly.

She held her breath, angry at the thought he expected her to let him kiss her, then cross that he did not even bother to try.

'Actually even if Pippa had a phone, which strangely enough she doesn't' he said slowly, as if to a child 'I couldn't have contacted her as there was no signal where I was working, in the middle of the mountains, and when I got to the airport the battery was bolloxed. Then I may have had the crazy idea that I would surprise her, by just turning up'

'What. You didn't say anything about that, how was I to know?'

He looked at her sadly. 'It doesn't matter now, it's too late. Although it would have been lovely to come back and find you were wearing that red dress for me instead of him'

'It was for you, you sodding idiot' she hissed at him

'Even if that's true, you soon changed your mind and moved him in with you'

He turned and let the heavy door slam shut behind him and Pippa.

Jen kicked the door in rage and stormed back to the cottage with Muffin.

The next afternoon Ted was home, and they spent the journey to the hospital discussing David and Patrick. By all accounts Patrick had been great company in Oxford but since he left there had been very little communication and he seemed distant when they did get a chance to speak.

'Maybe it is just the pressure of his work' suggested Jen, 'He simply may not have the time or energy to be everything you want or need'

'Oh, I don't know. How can you run so hot and then so cold? I think I am just recreational, something and someone to enjoy outside of real life, a distraction and novelty, but not important enough to really matter, not important enough to be missed'

Jen squeezed his hand

'You don't know that, he has a very stressful job, maybe he just has to compartmentalise his life to deal with everything'

'I honestly don't know, whatever it is, it makes me feel like

crap, it is always me chasing after him, suggesting meeting up and basically wearing my heart on my sleeve. I have decided I can't do it anymore, I am going to cool off and see what happens, see if he reacts to that, or even notices'
'He knows I am only here for a while, if he is really interested he will want to make the most of it, if he isn't then at least I will know what the score is, and can return home knowing I gave it my best shot'
Ted also wanted to explain to David about the misunderstanding of why he was staying at the cottage, but Jen was still fuming, insisting that he didn't deserve any explanation. Why should she prove herself, she had done nothing wrong?
When they arrived at the hospital Jen hugged Ted tightly before they got out of the car.
'I can't tell you how much I love having you here. I wish you didn't have to go back to Canada, I am going to miss you so much'
'Hopefully, you can come and visit me, you would love Vancouver'
'That would be amazing. When I was younger, I always dreamed of travelling, that was my plan, finish college and just go. I never thought for one moment I would just be living in the same small village all my life. So much for dreams I have never been out of the country, I don't even own a passport'
'Well its time you lived a little Jen, had some time for yourself, no-one could have done more for Laura than you already have, it's your time now, before I leave we should decide on a date for you to come over'
The following week Mrs Pendlehurst was moved to the Stroke Unit of the hospital, and they hoped there may now be some progress in her rehabilitation. Ted and Jen slipped back to their own routines, with Ted working in the office all day until visiting the hospital. It was a glorious summer, and they spent most evenings after dinner walking Muffin or meeting up with the other couples at The Plough.

Patrick did contact Ted a couple of times, but did not invite him back to London, nor suggest they make any arrangements to meet up. Occasionally they would see glimpses of David, coming and going at Millstone House, but he never approached them and did not seem to stay there for very long. He had apparently visited the hospital, but they had not seen him.

Jen started planning for Laura coming home for the summer holidays, although she was disappointed that it would only be for two weeks. The gallery had offered her full-time work during the summer and of course she did not want to be away from Fin who she had now moved in with as the lease on her room was coming to an end.

One day Ted received a call from the hospital. They wanted to arrange a meeting with the family to discuss her progress and the best course of action to take for her future wellbeing. Ted called Dorothea to discuss this and was surprised and rather relieved when Caroline offered to come to the meeting too.

Caroline arrived the next day, neither Ted nor Jen had met her before, although they knew a little about her background. She had worked for 30 years in Qatar as the personal assistant to the CEO of an oil company, only returning to England once or twice a year, and had never married. Now retired she lived with her mother in Lyme Regis.

Knowing all this Ted and Jen were both rather surprised when they saw her, she was not what either had been expecting. For some reason because of her career and family background they had both presumed that she would be a rather conservative type of lady, so they were amused when Caroline arrived in a red Porsche, wearing killer heals.

Jen waited anxiously at the cottage while Ted and Caroline attended the meeting at the hospital. She paced around her kitchen wondering again if she would be able to stay there much longer, and feeling the same panic rising in her chest.

She had been managing it so much better lately, the anxiety, the black thoughts, the tappings, but it was never that far from the surface.

It seemed hours before she heard Ted arriving back at Millstone and a few minutes later Caroline driving away. Ted walked in and sensing her disquiet hugged her tightly. 'Hey, it's okay, it's okay, everything is going to be fine' he assured her softly 'You are not going anywhere, its been decided that Aunt Rosemary is best coming home. She does not want to go into a care home and the doctors believe that she will be able to live at home as long as a care package and the right equipment is available for her. We have decided on the way home that it is best to move her bedroom downstairs, then once all the equipment is installed, a special bed, hoist, wheelchair, commode, etcetera she should be fine'

'That sounds good, I could always help'

'That will be great and obviously we need to do quite bit to organise the house, but you will not have to take on any more responsibilities than you already have, we are going to arrange for carers to come in twice a day and even better than that, Caroline is going to move in to organise everything and be responsible for her daily care when I have to go back to Canada. So not only are you safe here to carry on with your work and stay in the cottage, you do not have to worry about Aunt Rosemary. Caroline is going to be here looking after her and you can just carry on as normal. Isn't that great news, that solves all of our problems'

Jen was not fully convinced, but at least it was not the worst-case scenario, she had been given more time.

CHAPTER 15

By the end of following week Caroline had organised work
to start on rearranging the dining room into a disabled
friendly bedroom, as it was the most suitable room in the
house. It had double doors leading from the hallway and
patio doors opening onto the terrace and garden.
Workmen arrived to dismantle the large oak table to enable
it to be stored along with several of the dining chairs, the
dresser and smaller pieces of furniture in one of the
bedrooms and the attic.
Jen then cleaned the room thoroughly in preparation for
delivery of the hospital bed and the other equipment that
would be needed. As she worked the sunshine poured
through the patio doors filling the room in golden light.
She thought about the happy times the Pendlehursts must
have enjoyed over the years in the beautiful room,
entertaining friends, dinner parties and Christmasses, she
imagined them as a young couple, chatting and laughing.
The ghosts of those happy days seemed to linger in the
now empty room, soon Mrs Pendlehurst would be lying in
here, until the day she could no longer even do that.
Caroline wanted Mrs Pendlehursts bedroom as it was

above the dining room and she would be able to hear her better. Jen wondered why a monitor could not be used from one of the guest bedrooms rather than the intrusion into the master bedroom, but she did not comment.

She prepared the bedroom for Caroline as requested, stopping to look at the framed photographs of Mr and Mrs Pendlehurst, their wedding day, holidays, parties. Photographs she had seen and dusted hundreds of times, but now the images from long ago, captured moments of happy normality seemed far more poignant. She carried them down to Mrs Pendlehurst's new bedroom and placed them where she would be able to see them.

Ted only had a few weeks left before he returned to Canada. He needed to complete his research in Oxford so had booked into a hotel for a couple nights and was then travelling on to London to visit Patrick for two nights. Patrick had been far more attentive recently and invited Ted to stay with him, suggesting they needed to talk about their relationship and discuss their future. Ted was not sure whether to be excited or apprehensive, but whatever the outcome he needed to know where he stood before returning to Canada.

Caroline was arriving the day after he left, and they had decided it would probably look rather strange that Ted was living with Jen, so he had moved back to his old bedroom. Jen was sweeping the kitchen floor when she arrived.

'Ah you must be Jen' she smiled offering a beautifully manicured hand.

This was the first time Jen had seen Caroline closely. She guessed that she must be at least in her late fifties, if not older, she was petite, beautifully dressed and groomed. From a distance Jen thought, she would have looked quite stunning, but up close you noticed more that was wrong with her face, than what was right. Her hair was too blond, her teeth too white, her eye lashes too long and her lips too full for her age, there seemed to be very little movement in her face, little expression.

'It is a pleasure to meet you, both Edward and dear Aunt Rosemary speak very highly of you, I am sure we shall get along famously'

'That is kind of them, if there is anything, I can help you with you just need to ask'

'Splendid, shall we start with a tour of the house? It must be more than 20 years since I last visited'

Jen led the way through the hallway and started with the drawing room.

'Goodness me, there have not been many changes made over the years'

Caroline looked carefully at each room they entered, opening wardrobes, and looking out of windows, as if she were a prospective purchaser and Jen the estate agent. When they had finished the tour, Jen made them a pot of tea and they sat at the kitchen table.

'Now Jen I would like to thank you on behalf of the family for your wonderful kindness to Aunt Rosemary, visiting her in hospital every day far exceeds your obligation and duties and we really have all appreciated it'

'It has not been a problem at all, I have enjoyed it' lied Jen

'That is kind of you and as I say we have really appreciated you taking care of Aunt Rosemary when mother and I were unfortunately not in a position to do so. But I want you to know that I am here now and will be sure she receives the best of care'

'That's good, but if I am needed at all I am happy to help'

'Thanks, but you are going to be busy with this house, I think you are best concentrating on that from now on'

'Yes of course' said Jen a little taken aback

'I am not being unkind' said Caroline looking around the kitchen 'but I think you must agree with me that for a number of years Aunt Rosemary has left you in charge rather than taking charge of you'

'What do you mean?'

'Well let us be honest Jen, you only work minimum hours and minimum days and yet you receive a rather generous salary considering that you are also living in the cottage rent free'

Jen tried to stay calm, even though she felt her heart pounding.

'Well, those are the arrangements that suited Mrs Pendlehurst, they are the hours that she wanted me to work and the duties that she had requested'

'I do understand my dear, and I am sure that the arrangement worked perfectly for you both over the years, but you must admit things have been allowed to slide'

She looked at Jen and smiled, with her small, bright white teeth, but not with the rest of her face.

Jen fought back the angry tears that were starting to prick her eyes.

'Are you suggesting that I have been taking advantage of Mrs Pendlehurst?'

'Oh no Jen, of course not, please don't think I mean that. I fully appreciate that half of the house has been shut down as it was not being used, and that Aunt Rosemary liked to live a very simple almost frugal life. I also appreciate that she was never particularly interested in the house, far more concerned with her beloved garden, books and committees. It is not your fault dear; it is Aunt Rosemary who has not kept on top of things'

'What I am trying to say to you is that you need to be prepared for things to change. Please be aware that you will now be required to work your correct full time hours, as you are going to be far busier in the kitchen with our meals, more laundry, more cleaning, more shopping. We are all going to have to pull together and be a strong team. When Edward leaves for Canada mother will move into his bedroom. I cannot be in two places at once, so it is sensible for mother to move into here, and I am sure she and Aunt Rosemary will be wonderful company for each other, but that of course will mean extra work for the both of us, okay?'

Jen looked at her perfectly manicured red nails and

couldn't imagine what work they had ever done.

'Now would you please excuse me, I need to make a telephone call about the broadband connection to this house. Would you be a dear and take my suitcases out of the car and put them in my bedroom'

Jen spent the rest of the day and week doing her best to avoid Caroline. She was afraid of not looking busy, so desperately searched around for extra work. Cleaning out the fridge, oven, larder, under stairs cupboard, anything she could think of. She worried about leaving Millstone before the evening each day and used her lunch hour to walk Muffin. Her stomach felt it was in knots and at night she lay awake angry and anxious.

At last it was Friday and Ted arrived back at Millstone. She was so pleased to see him and as soon as possible took him to one side out of ear shot of Caroline and told him about their conversation, but he did not seem to take her worries seriously. She had hoped that he would defend her and confront Caroline about how unfair and unkind she had been, but he just assured her that she must have misunderstood and that he was sure Caroline would not have meant to be unkind, she seemed really nice and he was absolutely certain that not only would she care for Aunt Rosemary but that she would also look after Jen's best interests too, she stayed quiet.

Of course, Ted would be leaving very soon and she realised that he didn't want or need this added stress. He had come to England for a few months to work on his book and see Patrick but had unwillingly been caught up in a real life drama he had not planned for. As kind and caring as he was, it was only natural for him to want to leave all of this behind and get back to his own life. Who could blame him, she wished she could leave it all behind too.

It was not fair to burden him with her worries, she was not his responsibility and there was nothing he could really do, he would be going back to Canada in a weeks' time. It was also understandable that he was grateful that Caroline had

stepped in and taken the responsibility of their aunt from
him, enabling him to return to his own life.

On Saturday Jen picked Laura up from the train station.

'Goodness me' said Jen, admiring Laura's long dark
chestnut coloured hair 'This is new, I never know which
Lolly is going to get off the train'

'Do you like it Mum? I only changed it a couple of days
ago and I am still not sure, it's a bit of a dull colour for me'

'I love it, you look very grown up and it really enhances
your beautiful eyes'

'Thanks mum, you are always my number one fan, it is so
lovely to be home. It's funny I never know how much I am
missing you until I see you again'

Jen looked at her 'Is everything okay?'

'Yes of course, I am always soppy when I am with you,
come on get me home'

They had lunch and walked Muffin. Ted was calling in for
a cup of tea later but ended up staying with them for the
whole evening. Caroline had gone back to Lyme Regis for
a few days to organise the house before her mother moved
into Millstone the following week. Jen was so pleased that
she had booked these two weeks off work months ago to
spend them with Laura, especially now Caroline was in
charge.

Ted was so pleased that his stay in London with Patrick
had gone so well, he had been worried that Patrick wanted
to end their relationship, when in fact it was the opposite,
he was arriving the next morning to spend the last weekend
with Ted before his flight back to Canada on Friday. They
were all booked for lunch at The Plough, Katie was home
and at last so were Hugo and Henry, it was also Fliss's
birthday so they had booked the private room at the back
of the pub for the 12 of them.

When she booked it Jen joked that the private room was a
safety measure as Fliss was far too noisy at the best of
times and with the added excitement of her boys at last
being home, celebrating her birthday and no doubt

plentiful amounts of alcohol, it was simply unfair to unleash her onto the other customers.

Ted and Patrick came to the cottage to walk to the pub, Jen was a little surprised when she met him, he was not at all what she had been expecting. Ted had always spoken about him in the most glowing terms, so she was surprised that he was quite nondescript looking and seemed rather serious, even slightly awkward especially in comparison to Ted.

As always, having time together was lovely, these people were more than friends, they were her and Laura's closest thing to family she thought as she enjoyed the stories, jokes and laughter. Hugo and Henry had grown and matured so much since she had last seen them, Henry even having a full bushy beard.

He had always been a rough and tumble kind of boy, getting into scrapes, falling out of trees, coming home drunk or with tattoos, or often both. He was a very keen rugby player, always seemingly sporting a black eye or sprain of some kind. He had a gregarious personality like Fliss and entertained them with stories from his year travelling.

Hugo was quieter, more sensitive, always happy to be in his brothers shadow. He had taken his parents break up badly, and for a time they had all been rather concerned as he was obviously not coping well. He seemed distant, was struggling at school, shutting himself away in his room and very anxious.

Jen could relate to all of that and saw he was on a downward spiral that needed to be stopped. At the time Fliss was not in the right place in her own life to be able to offer Hugo all the support he needed, or maybe even notice how badly things really were. Jen had gently stepped in and spent a lot of time with him talking, walking the dogs, reassuring him and carefully encouraging him away from the edge.

Because of this Hugo and Jen were particularly close, in fact even while working abroad this year he would still sometimes text her. So it was especially lovely for her to see him, she was terribly fond of this bright, thoughtful, gentle boy who was now becoming a confident young man. They were all now adults, Henry, Hugo, Katie, Jonty and Laura, they were already the next generation, their parents work now done and no longer needed in the same way. Mike stood up and toasted Fliss on her birthday and the return of all the children to the fold, as he was talking Jen was seized by a terrifying thought as she looked at everyone around the table. Would they ever all be together like this again? Had this phase of their lives now run its course?

Ted then stood and made a toast, thanking them for their friendship and hospitality during his stay and assuring them how much he would miss them. Jen tried to save the moment in her normal way, mentally taking a step back and looking onto the scene to capture her happy moment, but something felt wrong, it felt more bittersweet than truly happy. She knew she was always unsettled by change, Caroline coming into her life, Ted leaving it, but there something more.

It was another stunning summer day, after lunch they sat in the pub garden until early evening, but Jen couldn't help feeling a sense of foreboding creeping over her. Something was not right, and she couldn't release the knot forming in her stomach. Was it Ted leaving her or the worry of Caroline as her boss, or was it the way Laura kept looking at her since she had come home. Something was not right. She knew Laura as well as she knew herself and there was definitely something going unsaid, something that Laura was maybe afraid to say, she had to give her time, but she dreaded what could be coming.

Patrick left on Monday morning and later that day Caroline returned, her car loaded with suitcases and boxes. On the following day, the equipment that was needed was installed into Mrs Pendlehurst's new bedroom and on Thursday morning an ambulance brought her home.

Once settled, Jen and Laura walked over to visit her. Jen had not seen her for over two weeks and noticed how thin she looked compared to when she had left the house in a different ambulance on that awful night, but she seemed happy and relieved to be back home amongst her own things and was delighted to see how the garden was progressing. Her bed faced the French windows giving her the best view of the new landscaping, the sunshine pouring into the room.

Afterwards Laura went riding with Katie and Ted asked Jen to have lunch with him at the pub they had been to on their very first walk together. As they walked Muffin through the woods and along the lane, the sunshine dappled the path, but the mood felt somber between them.

'Are you going to be okay Jen?' Ted asked, putting his arm around her shoulders as they walked along.

'I will be fine, I am just really going to miss you' she replied jokingly looking up at him with a sad face.

'I hate to think of you being lonely here. I know you have Fliss and Helen and they are great but they have their own lives, and now Peter is firmly on the scene Fliss is going to have less time'

'But what can I do about that Ted, it is just the way of things, I just have to make the best of everything and hope it doesn't get any worse'

Jen saw the genuine concern and worry on Teds face.

'Look Ted, I have loved every minute of your visit, it has been wonderful having you here, a very special time that I will always remember, but please don't worry about me, I will be fine. I was used to being on my own before Laura came along and to be honest I didn't think I would ever be able to say this, but I have gradually got used to being on my own again now she is at uni. They say people get used to anything eventually. Listen, we are going to stay in contact, so I will always have you to chat to'

'I just hate to abandon you, I so wish it had worked out for you and David'

'Well, it just didn't, and that bridge has been well and truly burned'

'I saw him you know, early Monday morning. I was showing Patrick around the garden and he was there'

'Did you? I guess they must be nearly finished, I haven't seen him at all'

'I talked to him for a while'

'Oh. How was he?'

'He seemed okay. I introduced him to Patrick. My partner'

'Oh, right, what did he say?'

'Not much, but I think it sunk in, he looked a bit sheepish'

'He is too stubborn to admit he behaved badly no matter what you said to him'

'Maybe you are as well Jen, too stubborn and too scared. Sometimes you have to take a chance in life, take a chance on people'

'Ted, you couldn't understand. I just want a quiet life for me and Laura, I don't need drama or stress, not from David nor anyone else. If there is someone for me in the future, which I honestly can't imagine, it certainly would not be a man like him'

'I'm sorry, I didn't mean to upset you, that's the last thing I wanted to do today. Look, let's forget all about it, let's just enjoy what time we have left'

Ted spent his last evening with his aunt and Caroline, calling in to say goodbye to Jen and Laura the next morning. Jen was so glad that Laura was at home with her for another week or his going would have been even harder.

'I'll be back' he said hugging her, 'Remember, you promised to come to Oxford with me some time, I have to come back to take you'

As the following week passed, Jen noticed small changes in Laura, she seemed quieter, slightly withdrawn, and pensive, making her even more apprehensive that something was wrong, but never finding the right time to ask her.

The bomb shell was dropped on their last evening together.

It had been another warm day and they were sitting at the table on the little patio at the side of the cottage looking over the wildflower garden, Muffin stretched out contentedly at their feet.

'Mum, I need to talk to talk to you about something' said Laura quietly, her eyes firmly fixed on the garden.

Jen tried to remain calm.

'Yes, darling, what is it?'

'Fin is going back to Australia. He wants to be near his son and there may be a job for him with someone he knows'

'Is he, well I guess that's understandable'

Jen held her breath.

'Mum' said Laura now turning to look at her 'He wants me to go with him'

'What?' said Jen now smiling 'You can't go with him. How could you? You have another two years of your course'

'I have spoken to them, I can suspend my second year until the following year'

'What? No, you can't do that, that would be crazy. You have worked so hard to get there, you can't leave now. Finish your course first, then you can go to Australia if you still want to. Two years will go so quickly, then if you still want to be with Fin, you can go out and join him'

'Mum, don't be ridiculous, I am not waiting for two years to be with Fin'

'Then let him go to Australia and he can come back a couple of times a year to see you'

'No mum, that won't be possible especially if he gets a job, he can't take that time off, and if he doesn't get a job he wouldn't be able to afford to keep coming back here'

'But all your hard work, your plans of what you want to do and be, what about all of that? When you come back you will have to start again, make new friends, find a job'

'None of that matters to me, nothing is as important as being with Fin'

'Lolly you are young, this is your first love, you don't know what you want, you may feel very differently in a couple of months'

'I won't, we want to be together, and Fin needs to be with his son'

'Fin is a grown man who should know better than dragging a teenage girl halfway across the world. If he thought anything of you at all he would consider what is best for you and your future and not just him. He should not be expecting you to drop out of university and possibly ruin your future just because he has suddenly grown a pair of balls and a conscious about his child'

She realised she was shouting and stopped.

'Look, I want the very best for you' she said quietly 'I want you to be happy and have everything you want in life, but there is a right time for doing something like this and it is not now. Please Lolly, don't throw everything away because of a man'

'What should I do then mum? Should I be sad and lonely like you, living your life through your daughter? I want more than that, I want more than you have. You always told me that I should be an independent strong woman, but that is the last thing that you are. Let me live my own life. I have chosen Fin, I want to be with him, wherever he goes and whatever he does'

Jen was shocked by the venom in her voice as much as the cruelty of her words. She had obviously been feeling this pent-up anger for a long time. They sat in silence for a few moments.

'When are you leaving?' asked Jen eventually.

'Middle of September, we need to save some money first'

Jen hung on to that slim bit of good news. There was time, maybe she would change her mind.

'I am going to need my birth certificate for a passport, do you have it?'

'I guess so. It must be somewhere'

'Shall I go and have a look for it'

'No, it must be in the loft somewhere, I will have a look for it over the weekend and send it on to you'

'I am sorry Mum, I didn't mean to say those things. You are a great mum and I love you very much and will miss you. I don't want to make you sad or disappointed in me, but this is what I want to do, I am not you, I am me. I may be making a mistake, you are right, but it's my mistake to make. I can't bear the thought of not being with Fin and I want to see Australia, I want to live somewhere else in the world.

I know you are happy here, you have never wanted anything more than this cottage and this village, but I don't want to just stay forever in Long Bridge. This is your world, not mine, I want something more'

'What?' Jen said bitterly 'You think I have never wanted anything more than Long Bridge?'

'No, you can't have, otherwise you wouldn't have just stayed here. If you want something else in life why not just do it, I will never just put up with things'

'No Lolly I hope you never have to, but not everyone has choices, most people have to just make the best of things, I truly hope you will never have to do that'

'Yes, I do have choices, and this is what I choose'

'Okay. Then there is nothing else to say I guess'

Laura put her arms around Jen.

'I am sorry if I have disappointed you mum, please try and understand, if we like it there and decide to stay you could come out too. There is nothing keeping you here is there?'

'Yeh we'll see'

'And I will try and come home as much as possible before we leave'

'Great'

'You do understand mum, don't you?'

'Yes darling, I understand perfectly'

Jen could not sleep at all that night, she lay awake for hours in the dark. She always knew that this day would come, she had been such a fool to have put it off for so long, but when was the time ever right? The past cannot be changed she kept telling herself, whatever happens it is too late now.

At daybreak she found the old biscuit tin that she kept under the loose floorboard in her wardrobe and opened it for the first time in years, searching through the small collection within. Removing Laura's birth certificate, she looked at it for a while, then folded it neatly and returned it to the tin and placed it back under the floorboard.

They both did their best to act normally over breakfast, as if nothing had been said. An hour later at the train station they hugged and went through their ritual goodbyes but as soon as Laura had left, Jen sat on the nearest bench, her legs felt weak, she felt nauseous. She closed her eyes trying to get her breathing to steady, trying to get her head around what had happened yesterday, what had been said and the consequences of what now needed to happen.

CHAPTER 16

After another sleepless night, Jen was glad to be back at work on Monday morning, she needed to be busy and hard work would fill the empty hours. She did not want to think about her or Laura for another moment, she needed distraction and exhaustion so that she could sleep.

Jen was now grateful that Caroline wanted her working more hours. Her days were full, cleaning, washing, ironing, shopping, and cooking lunch and dinner for all the household. Caroline's mother Dorothea had now also moved into Millstone, and Caroline had been right, she was great company for Mrs Pendlehurst.

They were quite similar in looks and mannerisms although Dorothea enjoyed her home comforts far more, she entertained herself with hours of television, reading, sudoku and puzzles, and loved her food, especially desserts, cakes and biscuits which Jen was happy to keep making. You certainly could not see Dorothea working in the garden all hours and all weathers as her sister had loved to do.

The household had found a new routine, carers arrived in the morning to wash, dress and lift her with the aid of the hoist into her wheelchair, she could sit up quite well with some supporting pillows, so on warm days she would be taken out onto the new patio to enjoy the garden.

She never complained about anything, not once, even though the whole process must have been deplorable for such a proud and private lady.

She needed assistance to eat, so a carer, or Dorothea or Caroline would feed her, and she drank from a plastic beaker like a small child, which was somehow the saddest sight of all. Caroline spent much of her time in the study, occasionally going out in the evenings when Jen would be on call.

Jen worked all day and walked Muffin every lunchtime and evening, no matter the weather. She felt such pent-up nervous energy, she just wanted to keep pushing and pushing herself physically until exhaustion took over. The weekdays were better than the weekends when she cleaned and scrubbed the cottage and walked Muffin for miles. She did not see anyone outside of Millstone, when Helen or Fliss contacted her she made excuses that she was incredibly busy, assuring them that she was fine, she was great.

Ted messaged her and she would reply with the same lies, absolutely fine thank you, busy and happy. She told nobody about Laura, her plans, their last evening together, or her fears. Laura called and messaged several times a week, firstly checking Jen was okay but later when she became concerned, rang to enquire more and more about information on the whereabouts of her birth certificate. Jen had told her that she could not find the document, she did not know where it was and so had needed to request another copy. Delaying tactics, but for how long?

The Millstone garden was now finished and looked wonderful, even before it had settled, matured and grown. It had previously been a very functional, unimaginative, soulless plot of land with its rectangular vegetable plots, rose garden, shrub borders, old crumbling greenhouse, fruit trees, lawn and discoloured patio.

Now the whole area seemed to flow and draw your eye

through the garden. The old patio had gone and, in its place, a sweeping terrace with steps down to a meandering path which wound its way to the ancient copse at the back. Smaller pathways branched out, one leading through a solid arched oak door to a walled garden within the walled garden, containing raised vegetable beds, a herb garden, new oak framed greenhouse and the orchard.

Another lead to a stunning cedar summerhouse with its own oak deck looking out on a wildflower garden surrounding a wildlife pond with a stone bridge that looked as if it had been there forever. There was now outside lighting, sunken into the terrace and along the path and lanterns on the summerhouse. It looked beautiful during the day and magical at night.

The deep sadness was the fact that Mrs Pendlehurst would never be planting in the new raised vegetable beds or growing her beloved flowers again. She would never be able to enjoy sitting in the beautiful summerhouse or pottering in the new greenhouse, it was all too late for her. The one consolation was that she did seem to enjoy sitting at the patio doors looking out on it.

Apparently David had visited when the work was completed and taken her in the wheelchair as far into the garden as she was comfortably able to go, and shown her a video of the areas she could not reach. He was going back to Italy for a month and wanted to be sure that she was happy with everything before he left.

Jen had seen nothing of him at all but remembered his invitation to accompany him to Italy on his next visit. That seemed a lifetime ago now. Had she really been that happy just a few months ago?

Two weeks passed and Laura was getting suspicious, she wanted to chase the delayed birth certificate herself. There was no more time to delay the inevitable, Jen telephoned her.

'I have you birth certificate here'

'Thank goodness for that, would you be able to send it

recorded delivery please mum?'

'No Lolly, I am going to come and see you on Saturday so that I can give it to you'

'You don't need to do that. As much as it would be lovely to see you, it's a long way, it will be perfectly safe sent in the post'

'No, I would rather hand it to you'

'Well stay the night then mum, we don't have a spare bedroom but there are plenty of reasonably priced hotels nearby'

'That would be lovely, but I need to get back, I can't leave Muffin. Can I come about 10 o'clock?'

'Yes of course, Fin will be at work then though'

'That will be perfect, I will come then'

Jen left first thing on Saturday morning and drove as if on auto pilot. She arrived early and rang Laura to tell her that she was in the car park opposite her apartment. Laura came down to meet her.

'Mum, are you okay? You have lost weight, you look really skinny'

'Maybe these jeans are just baggy. If I have it must just be walking Muffin'

They walked over to the large apartment block across the road, and climbed the two flights of stairs to the small apartment that Fin and Laura were sharing with their friend Matt. It was basic but clean and quite tidy for the number of people living in such small a space. Laura made tea in the tiny kitchen and they sat together on the sofa that filled most of the space in the sitting room.

'I cant believe you are here mum, sitting here on our sofa'

Without saying anything Jen passed Laura the envelope. She now felt surprisingly calm, almost an out of body sensation.

'Great, thanks so much for sorting this out, I will get it sent off straight away for my passport'

'You need to look at it Laura'

Laura pulled the certificate out of the envelope.

'What does it mean? Is this not my birth certificate?'

'Yes, it is yours'

'But who is Christine Merchant?'

'Your mother'

'What do you mean? Did you change your name?'

'No'

'Did you adopt me?'

'No, I didnt'

'Then what does it mean, if this Christine Merchant is my mother, who are you?'

'I am your sister.......well actually, I am your half-sister'

The room was silent while Laura processed the information, staring at Jen and then back to her birth certificate.

'What do you mean, is Christine Merchant is your mother too?'

'Yes'

'So, what happened to her, did she die?'

'I don't know'

'What do you mean, you don't know'

'She may be dead by now, I don't know, she was alive the last time I saw her'

'And when was that?'

'About 19 years ago'

'But why did I grow up with you and not her?'

'Because.... I took you away from her'

'What do you mean you took me away, why?'

'Because our mother was an alcoholic and a drug addict, and I knew exactly what your life was going to be if I left you with her. She was never going to look after you, she had no interest in you so I couldn't just leave you there with her'

'But you can't just take away a baby, surely someone must have noticed I was missing'

'For years I worried that the authorities may come looking for us, but gradually I decided that nobody really cared enough about either of us to worry where we were'

'But what about our mother, she must have wondered what happened to me, to us?'

'No, she would have probably been relieved not to have us there'

'What about my dad?'

'I don't know who he is'

'And your dad?'

'I don't know who he is either'

'Well what about social services, why didn't they help us, or help her'

'I am sure they would have intervened eventually, when her care of you and her lifestyle had been reported to the authority's enough times. Although she was very manipulative, she knew how to play the game and of course was given more money when she had a child, so she would have no doubt played them along for a while'

'Did you live with her?'

'When I was young, I did. They eventually took me into care when I was six or seven. Then later for some reason she wanted me back and they handed me over to her, but eventually the police came and took me away and I went back into care again'

'I can't believe you have lied to me all my life, why didn't you just tell me rather than leave it until now?'

Laura's eyes filled with tears

'I know you must be angry that I lied. Believe me I always meant to tell you, but the time was never right. Should I have told you at five years old or ten years old or fifteen years old? I knew that once I told you there would be loads more questions.

How old does a child have to be before they can be told that their own mother thought more of her next fix or bottle of vodka than of them. Be told that they were never wanted, never loved.

It was just too painful to have to tell you, I couldn't bear the thought of her still being able to ruin your life, to knock your confidence, force you to question who you really are.

I wanted you to have a normal life, to live with normal people, to be confident, happy, and proud of who you are. I never wanted you to feel like an outcast, to feel that you were not as good as anyone else, the unwanted mistake of an alcoholic. I don't want you to feel ashamed, or feel embarrassed of who you are, it effects your whole life, it hangs over you like a black storm cloud. Believe me, I know'

'But lying has been worse than the truth' said Laura 'I have spent my whole life wanting to know about my father, who he was, where he was. I wanted to know about our family, if I had grandparents or aunts, uncles and cousins. But you were always so closed off, so secretive, you made it too difficult to ask about anything, you always put up a wall and I did not want to upset you. A huge chunk of our lives was missing, a void only we seemed to have. No more lies. please, tell me now, I want to know everything, just talk, tell me about our mum, tell me about you'

Jen started slowly, talking as dispassionately as she could. 'Well, I guess that our mother was very troubled, she had her own demons, her own problems and consequently very little interest in for caring for me, but you don't realise that as a child, whatever your family situation is, it of course just seems normal. Looking back now as an adult I can see that there must have been something emotionally or mentally wrong with her, she only ever really thought about herself, or whatever man was around at the time. I learned very quickly to keep out of the way as much as I could and to fend for myself.

The only person I can remember showing any kindness to me at all as a child was Mrs Patel who ran the corner shop, if she saw me hanging around the street outside she would often bring me out some sweets or crisps, or if it was cold or dark she would invite me in and let me sit on a little stool behind the counter with her and she would share her lunch or make me a hot drink. Do you know, I haven't thought about Mrs Patel for thirty years, but she was lovely, she had older children who helped in the shop sometimes and I remember wishing the I could just stay there with her forever and that she could be my mum too.

I was eventually taken into care when the school reported me to social services, apparently, I was going through a dustbin looking for some food the other kids had thrown away. This added to the reports from some of the neighbours that I was often left on my own made them decide to take me away from her.

I remember the novelty of then having regular meals and clean clothes, but I still hated being at the children's home, in some ways that was even scarier than being with mum, at least I knew how to escape from her. There was no escape from the children's home, and some of the kids in there had serious problems, it could be really scary.

Then after a few years mum apparently got herself sorted out, she had stopped using, stopped drinking and wanted me back, I was about twelve then. I had never settled with a foster family, so they agreed and gave me back to her. It was okay for a while at the beginning when it was just me and her, but then she met this scumbag called Gary who quickly moved in with us and soon things were just as bad. They were both drunk or high most of the time and the place turned into a doss house for Gary's friends to sell their drugs and crash out on the sofa.

He lived with us for about a year, in fact the only bit of motherly advice I ever remember her giving me was about Gary, she said to be sure I kept my bedroom door locked as she had seen the way he looked at me. I had noticed the way he looked at me too, and the way he was always grabbing at me, especially when his disgusting friends where there, his revolting comments used make them all laugh. I don't know if she had seen him do that. Maybe, but of course, nothing was ever said.

They used to fight all the time so I either stayed locked in my bedroom or kept out of the house. There was a children's playground around the corner from that house so I spent most of my time there if the weather was okay, or I hung around the shopping centre if it was not, neither were the safest places for a young girl to be hanging around.

Anything could have happened, and there were occasions where it very nearly did, weird people know a vulnerable child when they see one.

One night I was in bed and there was screaming, that night it was worse than usual. I sneaked down to find Gary sat on top of mum, he was holding her hair and bashing her head up and down on the kitchen floor, her face and hair were covered in blood. There was a sharp knife on the worktop, so I picked it up and stabbed him in his back, then ran out of the house in my bare feet.

The police found me hours later at the playground and I was taken into care again. Nobody ever asked me about stabbing him, they maybe thought that mum had done it in self defence, and in all honesty the two of them were probably too out of it to know what had actually happened. Anyway, they both survived, I don't know how much longer they stayed together after that. It was years before I saw her again.

When I was seventeen and ready to leave the children's home a charity helped me find somewhere to live. I was appointed a case worker called Harry, who was just great, he found me my own little flat and I started a course at the local college. I had missed a lot of school over the years so sometimes I found the course a bit difficult, but I loved it, I loved it all.

For about a year I was really happy, I made friends, I had a place of my own, I even had a few boyfriends. I thought that once I had finished college and gained some qualifications, I would make a life for myself somewhere far away from there, hopefully abroad. That was my dream, to get away and put it all behind me.

One night I was in a local pub around Christmas time with a group of friends from college when there was a commotion outside. We looked out of the window and there was mum, stinking drunk, screaming and hitting out at a couple who were obviously in the same state. She was shouting and swearing at the other woman, pulling her hair and punching her and the man was trying to get between them to stop them fighting.

My friends were all laughing at them, of course I didn't say anything and sat back down quickly before she had the chance to see me, I was so ashamed. But before I sat down, I had seen that she was obviously pregnant.

I thought about what to do for a long time. In lots of ways it was none of my business, I had managed to get away from her and her world and was trying to find something better for myself, I didn't want to get sucked back in. But I couldn't ignore the fact that another child was going to have to go through the same as me, and that child was my brother or sister, my family. In the end I decided to make contact with her again, just to be sure the baby was okay. She was surprised to see me, happy when I said I would help her. I tried to convince her that you may be better adopted or fostered, but she was not having any of it. I think you were a bargaining tool, maybe to get the father to come back, or to get more money from social services, I don't know. Anyway, I brought her food, cleaned the house, got you a secondhand carry cot, blankets and some baby clothes.

I was at the hospital when you were born, I was the first one to hold you, bathe you and give you a bottle, you were gorgeous, perfect. Maybe I should have told the authorities that you were not safe, but I knew that even that option did not mean you were guaranteed to have a happy life. Who was to know where you may end up? I hoped that with my help she would be able to manage, plus selfishly by then I didn't want them to take you away from me either, I already loved you so much. I stayed at her house most of the time and juggled my final term at college with looking after you.

I didn't have anyone to talk to about the situation except Harry. My friends would not have understood, and I was too embarrassed to tell them the full story anyway. Harry was great and supported me in any way he could, he even helped me with the extra money I needed for you. After a short while though things started to slide, and I could see that she was back to her old ways.

She started going out more and I knew that she was drinking again so was constantly worried about leaving you with her, but one day I had an exam and had to go into college, she promised me she would stay with you. When I got back to the house you were lying in your cot screaming, the place was freezing, and she was nowhere to be seen. She had just left you, no doubt presuming I would be there eventually.

I fed and changed you and she still was not back, I was furious, so I made the decision to take you away from her. I had given her enough chances, by then I knew that she was never going to change. I couldn't leave you with her and I couldn't be sure social services could keep you safe, having been through the system myself. In the end I decided you were safest staying with me so I collected all of your things together, everything you would need and called the only person I knew I could trust, Harry.

Harry came and collected us. The flats where I lived were allocated for single tenancy only, so he helped moved us into temporary accommodation and then after a few weeks he found the position at Millstone House, he even drove us there, bless him. Do you know the saddest thing.....she never even came looking for you, I never saw her or heard from her again'

Laura held her hands 'Oh mum, you were even younger than I am, that was so brave, I cant imagine having to do anything like that or make those kinds of decisions. Was there no one else around who could have helped us, didn't we have any other family?'

'I don't remember meeting anybody, mum talked about her parents occasionally, mainly to tell me how lucky I was that I didn't have a father like hers, and that I had it easy. I remember our grandmother occasionally sending her money, she always referred to her as 'the poor cow' I don't think I ever met them though, I don't remember them at all'

Laura put her arms around her Jen.

'I am so grateful mum, you could have had such a different life, you have sacrificed everything for me. There I was putting you down for not doing more with your life, I am so sorry, I have been so selfish'

'You didn't know and anyway it wasn't a sacrifice, it has been the happiest time of my life at Millstone with you. I have always been terrified if I did the right thing though, I still do'

'What do you mean?'

'Maybe I was just being selfish wanting to keep you to myself? If I had reported mum and let social services take you into care, you may have had a much better life, been adopted by a loving couple and had a proper family. I have always been terrified that I let you down, I will never know if I ruined your chances for a better life by taking you.'

'I do have a proper family, I have you, no-one could have loved and cared for me more than you. I am so sorry I made you relive all that mum'

'Actually I have been horrified of the truth coming out for so many years that it feels such a relief, like a huge weight off my shoulders, I was always so scared you would hate me for what I did'

'Don't be silly, it just makes me love and appreciate you even more'

Later Jen drove back to the cottage feeling numb and exhausted but purged. That night for the first time in months she slept right through, not waking until she heard Muffin crying at the door to go out.

All the next day she sat around in her pyjama's feeling physically and mentally drained, but at peace with herself. She had told Lolly who she was and what she had done, and she had forgiven her. She understood and still loved her.

For the first time, Jen now wanted to confide in Helen and Fliss. They were good friends and she knew how odd it must seem to them that she never discussed her background, her past nor Laura's father, for all these years. She had carefully avoided the subject and they had generously respected that, even nosy Fliss. But Laura was visiting soon and would see Katie, it was only natural that she would want to discuss everything about her past with her best friend. It was time to stop the secrets and the shame, time for them both to move on.

She asked Helen and Fliss to come for coffee the following Saturday morning. Jen had been avoiding them for a long time, and was now inviting them together, it would be sure to make them suspicious that something was wrong. Helen was picking up Fliss on the way, so Jen was certain they would have been discussing the possible motive for the sudden invitation.

'Oh my good god just look at you'

Were Fliss's first words

'You look awful, you are so thin, whatever has been happening?'

Jen had worn her baggiest clothes to cover herself, but there was no escaping Fliss.

'I'm fine, I have just been a bit stressed lately but I am honestly okay now, I just want to talk to you both about something, honestly there is no need to worry. Come on, I will make us some coffee and we can go and sit down'

Jen told them about her childhood. There were some details of her past that had been too painful, too personal, to share with Laura for fear of upsetting her more, memories and terrors she had buried deep within herself, that she now shared for the first time with anyone. Fliss and Helen sat either side of her on the sofa like marble pillars supporting and giving her the strength to enable her to continue.

She told them about her fear of still being unsure, even after all these years, that she had done the right thing, or if Laura would have had a better life being adopted by a real family.

'You certainly cant be to blame nor be responsible for anything that happened to Laura, your mum or yourself, you were just a child' said Helen 'What you did and the life you have given Laura, has been amazing, you were so brave to face all that on your own, just look at her she is a real credit to you. And she does have family, she has all of us' They drank more coffee and as always, their shared humour made light of even this conversation.

'I was always convinced that you had been given a secret identity by the police or special forces' said Fliss 'that you were a fugitive, or had witnessed some gangland murder and they were hiding you and had erased your past. I even wondered if maybe it had been a case that Mr Pendlehurst had worked on and he had agreed to help keep you hidden away'

'No, nothing that exciting, but I am flattered you imagined me being such a colourful character'

'It explains another thing though' continued Fliss 'I never understood how you still had a great figure, why you didn't have the sagging arse and droopy tits like the rest of us. Now I know that you have never put your body through having kids it makes me feel so much better'

They hugged when they left and both told her to try and put some weight on and not to shut them out again. Jen felt a huge weight off her shoulders. When she walked Muffin in the woods later that day she enjoyed the beautiful colours of the leaves turning red and gold and the diluted sun that was still warm on her back. Laura would be home next weekend and then she was leaving for Australia, but it wouldn't be forever, hopefully she would be back before the summer by the latest, everything was going to be fine.

Maybe now it was time to build her own life, Laura was right she did live through her, and that wasn't fair. She was incredibly lucky, she had Laura, good friends, a lovely little cottage, her health, Muffin. Who knows, she could maybe start studying again, go to night school or find an Open University course that interested her. Maybe one day there may even be a man in her life. She would be fine, she had survived much worse.

CHAPTER 17

Laura stayed at home for a week, happy to find Jen more at peace with herself and they talked for hours. She admitted that she had felt incredibly guilty for leaving Jen to go to university and had nearly never gone at all.

'I felt your whole life was tied up with mine, and that you wouldn't cope without me being here, it was such a relief when you were absolutely fine and started making a life of your own, especially when you met Ted and David'

Jen did not tell her about the overwhelming loneliness she had silently suffered for the first six months, already feeling dreadful that she had unintentionally passed that guilt and burden onto Laura.

Fin and Laura were flying to Australia in two weeks, she would not see her again for months but even as they said their goodbyes there was not the usual feelings of panic. Jen didn't know if it was because she felt confident that Fin would be taking care of Laura, or that the demons of their childhood had now been released, she was just grateful that the blackness had eased.

Laura had persuaded her to visit them in Australia once they had found somewhere to rent. Jen had some savings, and it did sound an amazing opportunity, she would be able to fulfil one of her childhood dreams at last. They talked about travelling together for a few weeks while Fin was at work so they could explore more of the country. Jen promised to send away for her first passport and look at some dates once they had settled.

Life got back to normal, Jen worked at Millstone House during the week and made herself busy at the weekends, she sent away for her passport, looked into some evening courses that were starting in January, joined a yoga group that met in the village hall on Saturday mornings and bought a book about travelling in Australia. When she told Ted about her plans, he suggested that maybe they could meet in New Zealand when she left Australia and travel there together too, which would be perfect.

In a long email she told Ted about her childhood and that Laura was her half-sister, it seemed so easy to pour everything out to him. Since talking to Helen and Fliss, nothing had ever really been mentioned again when they were together. It did not feel that the subject had been swept under the carpet, they just seemed to want to tread carefully and not open old wounds, Jen didn't want to keep mentioning her past as it sounded like self-pity or self-indulgence, but she would have liked everyone to feel comfortable when talking and not purposefully avoiding the subject.

Ted on the other hand asked lots of questions and seemed to analyse her reactions, sometimes even pushing her for answers, which she guessed was the journalist in him. Because these conversations were often by email, even though picking at the old scabs could be painful at times, she could take everything at her own pace, sometimes needing time to digest his comments and questions, sometimes sending back a simple yes or no in answer and on other occasions ranting on and on for pages. It was therapeutic. Ted had suggested it would be really good for her to have some professional therapy, so she had visited her local GP and was waiting for an appointment with a counsellor.

Laura and Fin had started to settle in Australia and were loving it. Laura video phoned every couple of days, so they were actually talking more often now than when she was at university, she also sent photographs every day, the wildlife, the food, the shops, the views, everything was so different.

It was the first day of October when Caroline asked if she may talk to her when she arrived for work that morning. Jen followed her into the office and sat on the chair opposite the oak desk.

'Jen, I will come straight to the point. We could not have managed without your help over the last few months with the house and Aunt Rosemary. I also of course appreciate that you have been a very loyal employee for 19 years so believe me this is not easy for me to say, but unfortunately we are going to have to let you go'

Jen did not move.

'Sadly, we are now at the stage where Aunt Rosemary will be needing more specialised care. We also require a gardener as well as a housekeeper, so we have decided that the only solution is to be able to offer the cottage to either a full time carer or a husband and wife team to fulfil the duties of housekeeper and gardener. I know this must be an awful wrench for you, but now Laura has moved to Australia I am sure you will be able to find something for yourself easily, and of course you will be leaving with glowing references'

Jen sat completely still, heart pounding. She of course always knew this day would come, but right now it was as if a rug had literally been pulled from under her feet, she was falling, falling.

'I think three months seems to be the standard practice in these things' continued Caroline 'So I have put an official letter together for you asking that you vacate the cottage by the first of January at the latest. If you are able to find somewhere before that date, all the better. Why don't you finish earlier today so that you can get your thoughts together, I am sure it will be strange after all these years, but you must have always known this was not a permanent position and that Aunt Rosemary would not be here forever'

'Does Mrs Pendlehurst know?'

'No, we don't want to upset her any more than we need to, sadly she is no longer able to make decisions about her best interests or those of the house. I now have power of attorney and in the end, it is I who has to decide what is best for everyone concerned. I would appreciate it if you didn't mention anything, we do not want to upset her any further do we'

Jen rushed through her work, she needed to get away, needed to think, needed her lovely little cottage wrapped around her. When she at last got home she wandered through the rooms, the kitchen, the sitting room, the two bedrooms and bathroom. Not a huge space, nothing of luxury here, nothing that most people would think was special at all, and yet it was and always had been her sanctuary, the only place where she had ever felt truly at home.

Everything was so familiar, so much a part of her everyday existence, the very fabric of the life she had built here. The furniture, the photographs, the paintings, even the pots and pans and plates and mugs, everything suddenly felt so precious. She looked at it all with fresh eyes, now more than ever before appreciating what they had.

She lay on her bed, suddenly feeling exhausted, and pulled the duvet tightly around her, looking at the ceiling that even held memories. When Laura was little, she would often cuddle in bed and they would look for the horsey. They had noticed long ago that the light and shadows in the corner of the ceiling formed the shape of a horse's head between the curtain rail and wardrobe and had named him Dobbin. How can we leave Dobbin? Then the tears came, Muffin jumped on the bed and cuddled up closely. What was she going to do? She had some savings but certainly not enough to buy a property, and she would not have a job so there was no chance of a mortgage. She would not be a priority for social housing, and she doubted that she would be able to afford to rent anywhere in the village or even the area.

She would have to move much further away, where rents were cheaper and find work, even then would she be able to find somewhere to rent that accepted dogs, and if she did, how would Muffin manage if left on his own all day while she was at work, it would be awful for him, it would be awful for her.

There was no way that she would ask to stay with Helen or Fliss, she knew that they would do their best for her and may even offer her a room temporarily, but she could never put them in that position. The last thing she wanted was for people to feel sorry for her, for her to be a burden. No, the only resolution was to move away and start again, she needed a plan.

The first thing Jen did was to lie. She messaged Laura to say that she would not be visiting Australia until the following spring as Ted could not take any time off until then, and she hoped that Laura would understand that she would prefer to coordinate her holiday with the chance of also travelling in New Zealand.

Then she emailed Ted and told him that Laura had the possibility of some work for the next few months and would it be okay if they delayed their tour of New Zealand until the following year as that would fit in better. This gave her some breathing space before she needed to tell them the truth, the fact that she could no longer afford to go.

She simply could not confide in them yet, there was something inside her, maybe due to her background, or maybe as Ted said, her stubbornness, that hated showing frailty or provoking pity. She wanted to have first found another home, another job, before she told anyone about being given her notice. She could face the consequences of her lies after that.

Next, she started looking online for work. In an ideal world she would prefer not to be a housekeeper anymore, as she knew she would probably be lonely. It would be wonderful at some time to start a college or university course, but there was no chance of her doing that, she didn't have any qualifications they wouldn't accept a mature student with nothing to offer. So, housekeeper it was.

Of course, she knew that wherever she went it would be a struggle being on her own, it is far easier to make friends when you have children. People also said that it was easier to make friends when you had a dog. Dog walkers tend to be sociable and chat to each other, but the only connection she made from walking Muffin was meeting David when he was working on the Robinsons garden, and then in all honesty she had not noticed him.

But he had noticed her. David. She had not allowed herself the luxury of thinking about him for a long time, her life was too messed up, too complicated to involve anyone else. But she still remembered the feel of his hands on her skin, still remembered the way he looked at her.

Life could now have been so different. If everything had gone well and they had started a relationship who knows how serious it may have become by now, she could have been moving in with him in January instead of leaving on her own. Well, one thing was for certain, nothing was going to happen now, she may never even see him again before she had to leave.

She knew that studies showed daughters of women who had multiple relationships with different men tended to go down the same path. Jen was the opposite, it was not that she did not like men, she guessed she had just seen too many of them at their worse, and it had made her doubt their intentions. There had been a few boys at college, but they were just that, boys.

The online advertised jobs listed a few housekeeping positions, mainly in the major cities or abroad. There was no way Muffin would fit in at any of those, it needed to be in the countryside, but none of those offered accommodation. In the end she put together a sparse CV and forwarded it to the suitable agencies.

Those that replied informed her that she did not have the necessary professional qualifications for a housekeeper or cook, but they would consider putting her forward as a cleaner. They also said it was very doubtful anyone would accept a dog.

She decided instead to look for any part time courses to attend whilst doing a different job, maybe then she could qualify for university and study for a career. The problem was she would be leaving Muffin for even longer, presuming she could find somewhere to rent that would accept him in the first place.

The nights grew longer and the days darker as winter started drawing in. She felt herself slowly sinking again, sleeplessness and dark thoughts were taking over and the 'tappings' ruled her days once more.

She had started the counselling sessions but was not sure if she was wasting her time. What was the point of them? They may eventually help her to deal with her past, but how could they help with her future.

It was the first weekend of November. Before it got too dark Jen took Muffin to the woods, as they were walking back through the connecting fields, she noticed a group of teenage boys huddled on rocks near the stream. Muffin ran over to investigate them, his tail wagging, but they didn't see him.

Suddenly an incredible noise filled the air as they lit a firework, the bang was so loud and unexpected it stopped Jen dead. Muffin put his head down and fled back into the wood.

'Muffin, Muffin' screamed Jen as she watched him bolt into the darkness.

She ran after him, but there was no sign, she could not even sense which way he had gone. She stopped and listened, hoping to hear him in the undergrowth, but nothing.

'Muffin, come, come' she shouted now panicking.

Nothing. She walked their normal route, calling him.

'No, no, not this, not this, Muffin where are you?'

She was now crying so heavily she could hardly see where she was going. She continued searching, calling his name until it was completely dark, there was no moon, and it was now too difficult to find the path.

She managed to scramble her way out of the trees and rushed home hoping he may have returned, but no, just a dark little cottage.

She rang Mike and Helen and they promised to check the barns immediately and help her look for him in the morning. She rang Fliss who asked if she wanted her to come over and sit with her. No, she couldn't face talking to anyone, Hugo overheard their conversation and took the phone from his mum.

'Jen, send me a photograph of Muffin and I will put it on the village website and Facebook page. There are lost dog sites I can register with too, I will be sure to put him on all of them. I will print some posters and put them around the village in the morning too'

'Oh Hugo, thank you, thank you. I will come and help you put the posters up first thing in the morning if he isn't back'

'No, you stay there in case he comes home, mum and I can do it. Are you sure you are okay'

'Yes darling, thank you, I so much appreciate your help, thank you'

'Right well send me a photograph straight away'

Jen had plenty of photographs to choose from and sent one that was a good close up. She then walked down the driveway and stood there looking up and down the road. Then back up the driveway and around the gardens, then back down to the road. She did it until she was exhausted and bitterly cold. She felt sick worrying what may have happened to him, he could have been hit by a car, or stolen, or could be hurt and unable to get home.

'Please, please Muffin, please I need you' she kept repeating to herself.

In the end she opened the kitchen door and sat on a chair with a torch all night, watching, listening and praying for him to come home. At 9am the following morning Hugo arrived to tell her there were now 30 posters around the village, and the 'Have you seen Muffin' page had already been shared 48 times. Jen hugged him.

'Can I make you a coffee or tea Hugo'

'No, I am going to drive out to the other side of the woods near Farley, have a look for him there and put up some more posters in case he ran straight through, Mum and Helen have already been out for a couple of hours, they are asking people in the village to check their gardens and sheds. Mike is looking in the wood from his end.

Jen burst into tears again, she did not think she could possibly have any left.

'It's okay Jen, I am sure we will find him'

'Everyone is so kind, what would I do without you all'

'Go and sit down and try and rest, you must be exhausted, just let me know if there is any news and I will tell the others'

It was now pouring with rain, he would be so cold, thought Jen. She put on her wellies, pulled the hood up on her raincoat and for hours walked down the driveway to the road again, looking up and down as the traffic passed, then searched the garden again and again, nothing, all these hours that had passed and no sign of him, she knew it wasn't looking very hopeful.

Jen had just returned to the cottage when she heard a vehicle on the drive, it was David's Land Rover. She watched from the door as he got out, opened the boot, and walked towards her carrying something in a blanket.

Oh no, please, please no.

She ran out to meet them.

'He's okay, just shaken up I think, go and run the bath and we can clean him up and have a good look at him'

Jen ran upstairs, started running the bath and David followed her carrying Muffin. He lay him gently on the floor and unwrapped the blanket. Muffin lay there exhausted, he was soaked through, covered in mud, and shaking, his sad brown eyes watching her every movement.

'Oh Muffy, where have you been?'

She kissed him and buried her face into his cold wet neck

'How did you find him, where was he?'

'I saw the posters this morning, and just thought I would have a look. But I didn't find him, Pippa did luckily, nobody would have found him where he was, all tangled up in brambles in a ditch and the water rising with all this rain. Pippa was running ahead, and I saw her stop, her tail wagging furiously, and there he was, poor thing'

'I will never be able to thank you enough, I honestly don't know what I would have done if anything had happened to him.'

David put Muffin in the bath and they gently washed him together, checking for any injuries but apart from a few minor cuts and scratches he seemed fine. Jen then wrapped him in a warm towel and David carried him down to the sitting room and held him closely while Jen lit the fire and rang Hugo with the good news.

As the flames burst into life and started warming the room, they lay Muffin on the hearth rug and Jen rubbed him with the towel and kissed his head.

'Don't leave Pippa outside, she is the hero, you must bring her in too'

David brought in Pippa and the small room looked even tinier as she excitedly greeted Jen, her tail wagging wildly.

'Oh, you clever girl' said Jen, kissing her head too.
She bought the dogs in two bowls of food which they
demolished within seconds and then gave them a chew
bone each. They lay down together on the rug in front of
the fire contentedly.
'Dogs are amazing' said Jen 'They can go through all sorts
of pain and trauma and come out the other side unscathed,
untouched, the awful event seemingly forgotten. You
would think Muffin had just been out for a stroll looking at
how happy he is now, instead of nearly drowning in a ditch
and spending a night wet and cold and scared. It's a shame
people cannot be like that'
She could not stop herself from crying again.
David hugged her tightly and it was exactly what she
needed, some human comfort. She had not realised how
much she had missed human touch, Laura had always been
very affectionate, they would often cuddle up on the sofa
while they were watching TV. She realised how much she
missed it.
'Are you okay, you look exhausted, and you are so thin'
She did not want to let him go and leaned her head on his
chest.
'I have had a tough few months, but I am fine now'
'Are you? You don't look fine, what's happened?'
Jen did not answer and just stayed in his arms with her eyes
closed, shutting it all out.
'I am so sorry' he said 'I have been an absolute prat'
'No, it's not you. It is not your fault, in fact it is nothing to
do with you at all. But yes, I agree you are a complete prat'
'I know, I know, I have been a right shit. I am stubborn
and jealous and pathetic. I was so happy to get home that
night to see you. When I was in Italy I couldn't think of
anything else, then I walk in and see you looking so
amazing in that red dress with some other man, I was so
angry with you. But then when I spoke to Ted and he
explained everything I didn't know what to say to you, I
was so angry with myself, I knew I had completely blown

it. I know it was all my fault, I get a bit.......obsessive about things'

'I was happy to see you too and couldn't believe the way you over reacted. I have sometimes imagined what would have happened if I had not been dancing with Ted when you walked in, or if your phone had been working, or if you had been able to communicate like a grown up, everything could have been so different, but none of those things happened. It may be for the best now anyway, the way things have turned out'

'What do mean for the best?'

'Well, it's too late now'

'Why what's happened, are you with someone else?'

'No, I am leaving soon, I'm moving away,'

'Where are you going?'

'I'm not sure but have been given my notice. Caroline wants a couple, so she can have a gardener, or a full time carer, anyway I have to be out before the New Year.'

'Surely there is some other way, you don't want to go, do you?'

'No, not really, in fact not at all, but it's not my decision to make'

'There must be some way around it. Have you thought about your options?'

'I have thought about nothing else, it's constantly going round and round in my head, driving me crazy'

'What about you friends or family, what do they think?'

'I haven't told anyone, I don't want anybody to know yet, not until I get myself sorted out and have some kind of plan'

'You have told me'

'Well, I guess I'm not so worried about telling you, it won't affect you like the others. I know they will just start worrying and interfering and I need to sort it out myself'

'It does affect me, I may not be in your life but I still care what happens to you'

'That's very kind and actually it is nice just to tell someone else'
'I am happy to listen if you want to talk'
Jen pulled away and looked at him
'Are you?'
'Of course'
'It would be great to talk to someone, I am driving myself mad, but you mustn't tell anyone else I am leaving, nobody knows but me, you and Caroline'
'I promise I won't say a word to anyone I am happy to be able to help, firstly though are you hungry? I haven't had anything since breakfast'
'I'm starving. I'm afraid I don't have much in to offer you though'
'Right you stay here with the dogs, I'll go and pick something up then we can have a chat and try and sort you out'
He kissed her on the top of her head
'I hate to see you looking so sad and lost, there will be a solution, there always is'
He was gone for about an hour giving Jen time to have a bath and change out of the clothes she realised she had been wearing since yesterday. David came back with ingredients to cook spaghetti bolognese, 2 bottles of wine, cheese and biscuits and salted caramel ice cream and immediately started cooking while Jen sat at the kitchen table watching him.
He poured them both a glass of wine.
'Right, while I'm cooking I want to hear everything that's happened, start from the beginning'
Jen sipped her wine, which went straight to her head after not eating for more than 24 hours but made the conversation easier. David cooked and listened, occasionally stopping her to go over something she had said. She surprised herself by telling him everything, her childhood, Laura, Fin, Australia, Ted, Caroline and eventually why she now had to leave Millstone.

It was so good to talk rather than keep everything inside and she had to admit, he was a good listener. By the time she had finished David had put the meal on the table and they had started eating.

'Shit' said David 'You have been through all that and I have been down the road licking my wounded pride'

'It's not your fault, don't be silly, how were you to know'

'You're welcome to stay at mine, I have plenty of room. Lizzy lives in the apartment above the barn and me and Pippa rattle around a four bedroomed house on our own'

'No, that's truly kind, but I can't do that. We don't know each other, this is the most time we have ever spent together, or spoken civilly to each other, we may not get on and then I would be back to square one, having to find somewhere again'

'You could just be my lodger, just that'

'Could I really? In a perfect world I would be staying here, and we would get to know each other slowly. But even if things were perfect, it would probably still not be plain sailing. I know a lot of that is my fault, I am always going to struggle with relationships, I have trust issues, demons, I cannot even imagine being in a proper relationship with a man. As for you, let us face it, you are controlling, stroppy, stubborn and jealous. We would both be better with other people who were less complicated'

'That would be boring, but thanks for the character assassination'

'I need to find accommodation that I can afford to rent, a job to pay for everything, and hopefully have the time for some kind of course to gain qualifications. That's a lot to find in a less than two months'

'Not impossible, you firstly need to decide on the area'

'Yes, that part sounds doable, but then I have the problem of finding somewhere to rent that will accept a dog and the extra money to pay someone to look after him when I'm not there'

'Why don't you leave him with me?'

'What?'

'He could stay with me and Pippa until you get yourself sorted out'

'Really?'

'Having two is no more trouble than having one and Pippa would love it'

'You would really do that?'

'It no big deal, I have plenty of room, and Lizzy looks after Pippa when I go anywhere, I can't take her'

'That would be such a weight off my shoulders. If I knew he was being looked after for a while, I could just rent a cheap room near one of the college courses I have seen, and get a job to fit around it'

'There is only one condition, you have to promise to come and visit him lots'

'Thank you so much David, you don't know what a relief that would be. Yes, I promise'

'Hopefully, you won't want to just come back to see Muffin'

'No, it would be lovely to see you too'

David slowly reached across the table and held her hand, then lifted it to his lips, kissing her palm, then her wrist, without taking his eyes from hers. He walked over and leaning down tenderly kissed her mouth, her face, her neck, then pulling her onto her feet he kissed her passionately, pulling her body in tightly to him.

Putting her arms around his neck he lifted her, she wrapped her legs around him, and he carried her upstairs.

The next morning Jen awoke to the sound of heavy rain pelting onto the bedroom window and slate roof. She looked across at the man in her bed, then crept downstairs quietly to let the dogs out. Climbing back into the warm bed she snuggled up to his broad back.

She took a moment to captured the scene in her heart, hoping that when she was on her own again she could remember this exact feeling, the warmth of his body, his soft skin against her, his smell, the comfort of feeling so safe.

Later they sat in the kitchen with tea and toast.

'I've had an idea' David said 'I am going to offer a gardener to Caroline for free in exchange for letting you carry on living here'

'Would you be able to offer that?'

'Yes, I will get one of my team to do it, or even do it myself if it comes to that, whatever it takes'

'But that will put you out of pocket, I can't ask you to do that'

'Listen, if keeps you here, then it is well worth it'

'That's too much to ask you for'

'I want you to be here. Anyway, in the long run it will save me time and money, otherwise I will be having to drive all over the country coming to visit you. I will talk to Caroline in the morning'

Jen walked over and sat on his knee putting her arms around his neck.

'You would really do that for me?' she kissed his mouth gently 'Thank you'

'Of course, I would do that for you, I want to look after you' he said kissing her back

'Do you think I need looking after?'

'At the moment yes, and you deserve to have someone looking after you. What do you want to do today?'

'Stay right here, sat on your knee and in your arms'

'Okay well we can stay here as long as you want, but then why don't you go and get dressed, we can stop off at mine and leave the dogs with Lizzy, I'll get changed and we can go and eat somewhere. I don't want you to get into the habit of me cooking for you every day'

'Okay, that sounds a good idea too, give me half an hour to have a bath'

'Shall I come and wash your back?'

'Ooh that sounds perfect'

They arrived at Meadow Farm Nursery, David opened the gates from the car, and they drove down a long concrete road to a Victorian farmhouse nestled in the bottom of the valley. He drove into a courtyard with barns on three sides, one was open fronted to park the vehicles, the second an office with an apartment above and the third was storage for gardening machinery and equipment. To the side of them were long neat rows of poly tunnels.

David parked the Land Rover in the first bay and they went through a side door to the house, walking into a boot room with a dog bed, storage shelves and boiler room. This lead through to a large kitchen with an old pine dining table in the middle and a rug in front of an Aga.

'I will just go and get changed, make yourself a drink if you want, or have a look around'

Jen walked through to the sitting room. She could have fitted her cottage into here three times she thought. It was a lovely house, solid, comfortable and homely, she noticed that there were lots of photographs of families and children. Were they his she wondered, had he been married, she had not even thought to ask.

'You have a lovely home' she said, when he returned 'Such lovely family photographs too'

'Thanks, yes I have three sisters and lots of nieces and nephews. In fact, you are about to meet one, I have asked Lizzy to pop over'

Lizzy arrived within a couple of minutes, she was maybe a few years older than Laura.

'Hello, lovely to meet you Jen, I hear I am looking after this little chap' she knelt down by the rug that the two dogs had already claimed and made a fuss of them both.

'That's very kind of you, I hope I am not putting you out'

'Not at all, it's just as easy to kick about here as it is at my place. If the rain stops, I will take them both for a walk in the field'

David drove them to an old, thatched pub with a roaring fire and real ale where they found a quiet table for two in the corner. It was getting dark by the time they got back to David's house and Lizzy diplomatically made her excuses and left when they walked in. The dogs had been for a walk, had been fed and were now lazily stretched out in front of the Aga. Jen was so pleased to have found a place for Muffin to stay that he would love. Would he ever want to leave though, she wondered?

'Why don't you stay here the night, it's a shame to disturb them now' David said nodding towards the dogs. 'In the morning I will get you back in plenty of time for work and then I can talk to Caroline'

He stoked up the log fire while Jen made them coffee and they curled up on the sofa together.

'This is lovely' said Jen 'Thank you for such a perfect day'

'This is how it could always be' said David

'Let me just enjoy this moment, this day, I manage better that way. I have loved today and of course I am worried about the future, terrified, but I need to build a life of my own to feel really safe, I hope you can understand that. I can't just risk relying on someone.

I have been in a panic since Caroline told me I had to leave, but sometimes you need your life to be shaken up so that you are forced to make changes that will hopefully make it better in the long run. Maybe this is one of those times, I can only hope it is.

What would happen if things didn't work out between us and you wanted me to leave? I can't risk that, I will never be happy until I feel secure in my own right, independent. If Caroline is happy for me to stay when you ask her tomorrow, then maybe that is fate. I will live and work there until they no longer need me, and we can see what happens between us. But if I must leave, hopefully we can still see each other. Besides, you are holding my dog to ransom'

'That sounds very sensible' said David quietly 'but you might go off and make this wonderful life for yourself and meet someone else, someone who is a part of that new life'
'And you may meet someone else too' said Jen 'In which case we would know that it's not meant to be. You may meet someone younger, someone you could have children with'
'Let's not worry about all that tonight' said David 'Let's just hope Caroline can be persuaded in the morning, you are here with me now. Come over by the fire and lie down beside me'

CHAPTER 18

The next morning, they arrived at Millstone early, David went to look for Caroline while Jen changed her clothes. She was just making them tea when David walked back in. 'What's the matter? She asked, seeing his expression 'Did you talk to Caroline?'

'I did, but something has happened I'm afraid. Rosemary Pendlehurst died last night'

'No. Really? Oh, my goodness, I knew she had been looking frail over the last few weeks, but I never imagined she was that bad, oh how sad, poor Mrs P'

David put his arms around her.

'Apparently she had another stroke yesterday evening and died before the ambulance arrived'

'Oh no, I must go over and see if I can do anything to help'

'Sure, I will talk to you later'

Millstone was unusually still, dark and quiet. Mrs Pendlehurst had liked to listen to Radio 4 during the day and it had become a constant background noise to the house. Normally there would have been carers coming and going at this time of the morning too.

She walked through the kitchen and hallway and found Caroline in the study.

'Good morning Caroline, I am so sorry, it must have been an awful shock for you and your mother, it was so sudden'

'Yes it was, thank you Jen, poor mummy is terribly upset, but we are both so glad to have had this extra time together with dear Aunt Rosemary, and to have been here for her at the end'

'Yes, I am sure she was really grateful to have you both here these last few months. Is there anything I can do to help? Have you both had breakfast?'

'Mummy is having a lie in, she didn't sleep well last night and I would just like a coffee thank you.

I am going to get the hospital bed and other equipment removed from the dining room hopefully within the next few days and have the dining table reassembled, so would you please concentrate on getting that room back to normal as soon as possible.

I have also ordered packing boxes which should arrive this morning so could you please organise Aunt Rosemary's bits and bobs in that room first, then later today when mummy feels up to it we will start going through the clothes and other personal processions, maybe you could then help us with that'

'Yes of course, I will go and make your coffee'

'Oh and Jen' said Caroline as she was about to leave the room 'This morning David asked me if you could stay on here, some idea he had about supplying a gardener in return for your accommodation. But I am afraid with the loss of Aunt Rosemary we will not need any staff in the future, we have already decided that once we have sorted out Aunt Rosemary's affairs and held the funeral, mummy and I will be returning to Lyme Regis and Millstone will be sold.

I am unable to talk to Edward until later today with the time difference, but we did briefly discuss the possibility of this situation happening before he went back to Canada and as beneficiaries of the estate we both agreed that it is for the best, as neither of us wish to live here. So I hope

that you are still able to vacate the cottage by the first of January as the house will go on the market in the new year, as you will appreciate, we do not want any sitting tenants'
'Yes of course, I understand perfectly'
So back to plan A thought Jen, well at least she now knew. It was no good panicking she told herself, there was now a glimmer of light at the end of the tunnel. She didn't have to worry about Muffin and Laura was settled in Australia at the moment, so she was perfectly capable of finding somewhere for herself that was cheap to rent, find some work and look into a college course.

It may turn out to be the best thing that had ever happened to her, it may be the start of something exciting. Jen always remembered and clung to something a teacher, Miss Kendal had told her once long ago, that she was a quick learner and could easily be top the class if she put her mind to it. Miss Kendal wasn't to know that she had more pressing things to think about in her life at the time.

She was happiest there and was always sure to get herself up and into class before her mother was even awake, in case she delayed her. She hated the school holidays when she would just hang around the estate or the children's playground all day no matter what the weather.

Miss Kendal's kind words meant more to her than she would have realised, they had always given her hope of what she may have been capable of if she had been able to enjoy a normal childhood with the luxury of just worrying about her school work.

She messaged Ted to say how sorry she. He responded later that day to tell her that once the date of the funeral had been confirmed he would be back for a week and looked forward to seeing her again.

Jen worked hard over the next few days helping to go through, organise and pack over 50 years of a family's life. Each drawer, each cupboard, each box was so sad to look through. Letters, photographs, mementos, books, clothes, jewellery, diaries. Lives lived to the full, lives so entwined with each other and others.

Their significance as someone's child, sibling, friend and partners to each other once so vibrant, so important to one another, a shared history, was now gone, just a memory in a black and white photograph, a saved Christmas card, an inscription in a book.

Nobody who was left would know the stories behind their possessions, the importance of the mementos they had saved and kept close to them for over 70 years. Soon nobody will even mention their names.

In the end no matter how you live your life in happiness or sorrow, your passions, fears, hopes, and ambitions, all that's left is stuff for other people to deal with. A lifetime of keeping things that are important to you are either an agony of emotions to those left to sort them, or an inconvenience.

Each day highlighted the fragility of life and the uncompromising fact of death, but it did strangely give Jen some inner strength. Acknowledging that in the grand scheme of things, each of us was a tiny insignificant link in the chain of humanity, only truly important to the adjoining links, made her feel it was senseless to live her life with so much fear.

In the end this was how everybody ended up, a few boxes of memories that after they died meant nothing. Why worry what the future would bring, she was healthy and still young enough to make a life for herself, it was time to grasp what she had with both hands, she had wasted too many years being fearful of life.

The good clothes were packed up for a charity shop. The jewellery and Mrs Pendlehursts family photographs and family possessions were carefully packed in boxes to go to Lyme Regis. Mr Pendlehurst's watches, wedding ring and personal family photographs were put in a box for Ted. It felt strange splitting a marriage into separate boxes, photograph by photograph, possession by possession.

When Jen was not at work she was gradually going through

her own belongings, trying to be ruthless and keeping just the most important items. David had offered her some space in one of the barns to store what she wanted to keep but would not be able to take, which again was very much appreciated. She had decided the larger items of furniture would have to go to a charity shop and would organise for them to be collected when she had a date to leave.

Fliss had come to see her on the Monday evening after the news had spread throughout the village. Jen told her about David, about having to leave the village and about David's offer to live with him.

'How did all that happen in the few days since I last saw you? I think you are right though, not to move in with David, it is all far too quick. I think you should live with me. Hugo is moving to London after Christmas, you can have his room'

'That is so kind of you, but I honestly don't want to put on anyone. I really need to find something of my own now and stand on my own two feet, to make something of my life for me'

'But what am I going to do without you? I am going to miss you so much' said Fliss hugging her

'Not as much as I will miss you' said Jen fighting back tears 'You have been such a good friend, you and Helen have been the only true friends I have ever known'

'You must promise me' said Fliss wiping away tears 'that if there is anything you ever need, or anything I can help you with, you will let me know. And you must come and stay with me whenever you get the chance, and I will of course visit you too. Why don't you come to me for Christmas? It will just be the boys and me, Peter is seeing his children'

'Thanks, can I let you know closer to the day, its weeks away yet and my heads all over the place, the last thing I am worrying about is Christmas'

'Of course, but please know I am always here for you whether you need a bed, money or help of any kind, I want to help, I love you to bits, you know that'

When she left Jen's new resolve to be stronger started withering away and she felt the panic rising. How am I going to cope, how will I manage on my own? Will I be able to make new friends?

On Friday evening she drove over to David's house with Muffin and a weekend bag. There was a lasagna cooking in the oven, a bowl of salad and freshly cooked garlic bread already on the dining table.

'That smells delicious' said Jen as she entered the kitchen

'Well I must admit Lizzy guided me, but I would like to think I am a bit of an expert lasagna cook now'

'You didn't have to cook for me' said Jen moving into David's outstretched arms 'I could have made us something'

'No, you have been cooking all week, anyway I am trying to fatten you up'

'I am trying to eat more, I guess my IBS has been triggered a lot lately, and then I just don't want to eat'

'If you stayed here that could all change, there wouldn't be any stress in your life'

'I am leaving. I am not moving in here, please I have already explained that lets just enjoy what time we have'

'Yes okay, but I was thinking, why don't you come here for Christmas, Lizzy's parents and her brother and sister are coming, it would be great to have you here, you could meet everyone'

'Um, well let's see, Fliss has already invited me to hers and I wouldn't want to let her down now I have accepted her invitation' she lied.

They had another lovely weekend, on Saturday they visited a pretty market town, had lunch and shopped, then cooked together in the evening, on Sunday they walked the dogs along the river and had a pub lunch. When they got back to Davids Jen collected her wash bag and clothes together.

'What are you doing, you don't have to go now, you could go back in the morning' said David

'I have some things I need to do this evening'

She suddenly felt that she needed to leave, to get back to own home. Being so close with someone for 48 hours had started to make her feel jittery, almost claustrophobic, she needed her own space. It was confusing, they obviously had feelings for each other, and she loved the intimacy, the feel of his arms when he held her, his body wrapped around hers, his touch.

They also seemed to enjoy doing the same things, but something was not right, was he too needy? Would he smother her, devour her and then spit her out? Or was she just pulling up the draw bridge, not letting him get too close, not allowing herself to be too comfortable, too vulnerable.

There needed to be some distance between them. As much as she longed to enjoy their time together, there was something stopping her taking that next step, that was making her feel guarded.

Jen avoided David for the rest of the week, making excuses about being busy. She used her spare time researching college courses and rooms available to rent. She also talked to Laura, who knew about Mrs Pendlehursts death but not yet about them losing their home, she decided that was going to be a conversation for another day. On Thursday evening David turned up unexpectedly.

'I have missed you' he said walking in and kissing her passionately 'Haven't you missed me?'

'Yes, of course I have' she answered, melting to his touch.

'Then why have you not called me?'

'I have just been so busy, in fact I have a really busy day tomorrow, Ted is flying in on Saturday and I need to prepare everything at Millstone for his arrival'

'Okay, well we don't need to go out or anything, I could get us a takeaway?'

'Actually, I am really tired, I was going to have an early night'

'Is that an invitation or a dismissal?'
'Well I guess we could go to bed, but maybe its best if you don't stay'
'So you want sex, but then I must leave'
'No, I didn't mean that'
But she was lying and they both knew it. It was exactly like that. When he was holding her, touching her, she felt wonderful, she felt like someone else. But when they were together the rest of the time, she was unsure of him and of herself. For some reason the more time they spent together, the more he made her nervous, she couldn't relax. His passion for her, his seeming adoration, could not be real, how could he be that infatuated with her so quickly? Soon he would realise that she was not worthy of all this attention and leave her. She knew it was never going to work out, it was just a matter of time before he worked that out too. The longer this fantasy went on the more unbearable that would be. One day he would really see her, and she would recognise the disappointment in his eyes. But there was Muffin. She could not upset David, or he may not look after Muffin for her.
'I think it is like that' said David, obviously hurt
'No, its fine, I am probably just a little tired, come on, let us go to bed' she took his hand.
'No, if you're tired you get some sleep' he walked out without another word.
It is for the best, she told herself, the longer it goes on the worse the ending will be.
The next day she prepared Ted's bedroom and baked his favourite almond cake, but in the afternoon, she received a message from him to say that he would be staying in London until Tuesday. She was so disappointed, she had been looking forward to having some time with him, but of course he wanted to spend as much time as possible with Patrick while he was here.
She used her free time over the weekend to empty the loft

in the cottage. They had lived there for over 19 years so there was a lot to go through. It was like sorting out Mrs Pendlehursts belongings but even more painful for her. It had been terribly sad that there was nobody to really care about Mrs Pendlehursts keepsakes, but these boxes were full of mementoes that still meant a huge amount to her and Laura, but she simply could not keep everything.

In the end she decided that she would allow herself two boxes of keepsakes and the rest she would give to the charity shop or throw away. This was practical, but so, so difficult. She brought down and emptied each box in turn, carefully laying out all the items on the coffee table and sofas. Two of the boxes were full of Lauras old toys, teddy bears, dolls, puzzles, books.

Each one was precious to them. She managed to reduce the two boxes to one. The remainder saved for the charity shop. Okay how were all the other boxes going to be reduced to the one remaining allocated box?

Next was a box of Laura's clothes from when she little. Her first pair of wellingtons, a favourite fur hat that had ears like a bear, a beautiful blue taffeta party dress. Why had she kept all this, she was now thinking, if she had just given them away when they were outgrown they would have been forgotten about, and she wouldn't have to do this.

She decided that in the future there would be no more memory boxes, what was the point of them in the long term? Eventually she managed to fit the tiny wellington boots and taffeta dress in with the saved toys and put the rest in a bag for the charity shop.

Laura's artwork was in the next box, Jen looked at each piece with fresh admiration, she was so talented, again she wondered where her natural gift came from. This would have to be the second saved box, she couldn't throw any of it. Two other boxes contained odd bits of household objects, a vase, a teapot, old picture frames, cushion covers, glasses, ornaments. They could all go.

The last three boxes were Christmas decorations, this was going to be hard. So many of them had been made with Laura, so many memories of happy times together. This year there would be no decorations put up, christmas was cancelled. She had already decided to decline both of the offers from Fliss and David, in fact Helen had also been questioning her about her plans.

She had decided that to tell her friends that she was going to David's house and tell David that she was going to one of her friends. All she wanted to do on the day was to take Muffin for a walk in the morning and then sit by her fire in her cottage for one last time and be thoroughly miserable, she needed to do that. None of them would have understood, but that is what she needed to do.

The last thing she wanted was to have to pretend to be jolly and she didn't feel that she needed to be, just to please everyone else. What about next Christmas, where would she be then? She could not even imagine.

In the end she broke her own rule to allow for a box of Christmas keepsakes. She would keep them in the boot of her car if David didn't have enough room. The rest of the contents, fairy lights, candle sticks, table ware, were packed with the other charity donations.

CHAPTER 19

The funeral was arranged for the Wednesday. Jen had prepared the house for the wake and Caroline had organised the caterers. Ted had eventually arrived from London late on Tuesday evening. Jen had been listening for his car on the gravel drive and waited impatiently for him to come to the cottage to see her.

He arrived twenty minutes later. She was so pleased to see him, to be scooped up in one of his big bear hugs.

'Come in, come in'

He walked through the kitchen and into the sitting room, immediately noticing the packed boxes.

'You have started packing'

'Yes of course, I couldn't keep putting it off, I leave in just over three weeks so I have had to make a start, it's surprising how much stuff a little place like this can hoard'

'What are you going to do with everything?'

'David has room in his barn for some of the boxes, but anything I don't actually need at the moment will be going, some to the charity shop and the rest will just have to be thrown away. I have found a room to rent, I think, although I have not actually been to see it yet, but it doesn't look too bad on their website and the rent is reasonable, so I am viewing it next weekend hopefully so that I can have a look around the area, it's about three hours away, so I am hoping I can do it all in one day.

All of the furniture here will have to go, nothing is of any real value to sell, and I cannot ask David to store sofas and beds. I did look into renting a small storage space, but it was so expensive that I have decided it is not feasible and have organised a charity to collect it after Christmas. I will just have to buy things as I need them when I hopefully have a place of my own one day.'

He looked at her 'Jen.....'

'Please Ted, please don't worry, and please don't make any fuss, it's not the end of the world, there are many people worse off than me. I have started to accept what I need to do and just get on with it and stop feeling sorry for myself. Who knows it could be the beginning of something wonderful, that's what I keep telling myself, and I really need you to be positive for me too, it will make it easier.

It is so good to see you, let's just enjoy the time you are here and not worry about what is going to happen next year. Now can I make you a drink?'

'No, I'm sorry I had better get back, Caroline wants us to go through everything for the funeral. I just popped over to say that I am here and that I will see you tomorrow okay. We can talk then'

'Okay sure, of course, I will see you tomorrow' It was hard to hold back the tears, she had been so looking forward to seeing him, to have someone to talk to, she had been counting down the days all week.

'Are you sure you are okay?' he asked squeezing her shoulders

'Yes of course, I will see you tomorrow'

And he was gone again.

The next morning Jen went to Millstone early to check that everything was ready for the caterers and visitors. She swept the floors and covered the dining table with a snow white cotton table cloth, carefully arranging the plates, napkins and cutlery. She talked to Caroline to ensure that she was happy with the preparations, but didn't see anything of Ted at all, apparently, he had left Millstone first thing that morning.

Once everything was perfectly in place, she went home, bathed, and dressed in black trousers, a white shirt and black cardigan, she would look like one of the caterers, but that was fine. She knew her role for the day, even though she had spent far more time with Mrs Pendlehurst than any of the family present at the funeral, she was still just staff. She dried her hair, deciding to pin it up so that it looked tidier and put on some make up. Then she wrapped up warm against the bitterly cold wind and walked to the church which was already quite full.

Finding Helen and Mike she sat with them and after a while Fliss joined them too. The family, Ted, Caroline and Dorothea arrived together a few minutes later and sat solemnly on the front pew. It was lovely to see so many people in the church, friends and colleagues from committees and groups that Mrs Pendlehurst had given so much of her time to over the fifty plus years she had been involved with the village.

Reverend Jackson conducted a very moving service, and spoke with fondness and respect about her diligence, loyalty and self-sacrifice serving the local community. After the ceremony Reverend Jackson and the family followed the undertakers carrying the coffin through the church, out of the ancient oak doors and onto the graveyard and the family plot where Mr Pendlehurst already lay. The burial was being witnessed by family members only.

As soon as they had left the church Jen stood and made her way quickly to the door, she needed to be at Millstone before people started arriving.

She had not noticed him, stood at the back of the church was David, her heart leapt for a moment when she saw him, he looked so handsome in his charcoal suit. As she approached him, he moved forward to talk to her.

'Sorry David' she said more abruptly than she intended 'I have to rush back and make sure everything is ready. Shall I see you there?'

He nodded impatiently.

She hurried back to Millstone kitchen, hung up her coat and had a quick chat with the caterers to confirm everything was in order. There were already trays of sandwiches and cold finger food laid out on the dining table and she could smell the hot buffet warming in the oven awaiting the guests. The glasses were ready on the trays for serving wine and sherry and the china cups and saucers prepared for the tea and coffee.

People started arriving, Mike and Helen did not come back to the house but Fliss did and Jen was grateful when she naturally took over the proceedings with her normal flair while they awaited the family to return.

Each time the door opened Jen looked up hoping to see David, but he was the last to arrive, then stood awkwardly at the door. Caroline talked to him for a while and then Fliss, but he did not look like he was encouraging them, and they soon moved on to someone else.

Caroline had asked Jen to circulate with the tray of sherry and she had been captured by the Carson sisters, two elderly ladies who ran the horticultural society, both very sweet but incredibly talkative, they both wanted to tell Jen at length of their fondness for dear, dear Rosemary and discuss her tireless commitment and passion to the village horticultural society.

Jen noticed over their shoulders that David was staring at her and signaling for her to come over, but it was difficult to make a polite escape. Eventually he walked over, took the tray of drinks out of Jens hands, placed it on the nearest table and asked the Carson sisters to please excuse them.

He took her arm and guided her out of the room and into the study.

'Whats going on?' he asked

'What do you mean what's going on? You know whats going on, I am working'

He leaned against the edge of the desk.

'You look very smart by the way' she said lightly, smiling 'Very handsome in your suit'

But he didn't respond, he searched her eyes looking for something more.

'Look' he said eventually 'I don't want you to be nice to me because you want me to take care of your dog, or store some of your belongings. That will never be an issue I will do that for you whatever happens. But don't give me all this shit. If you don't want a future together then that is up to you, but just tell me because there is no way I am going to spend another year chasing around after you like a soppy teenage boy. I cant do that anymore, I need you to tell me whats going on'

Jen looked at her hands 'I'm sorry that you feel I am messing you about, honestly I am not meaning to, you know I am very fond of you'

'You are very fond of me. That's kind of you, you sound like an old aunt. Is that it? You have not contacted me all week, you hardly bother to answer any messages I send and when I suggest us seeing each other there are always excuses'

'I cant help that David, I am busy. I am working and packing and when I am not doing that I am looking for somewhere to move to in three weeks, there are a lot of things I need to organise'

'Thats just an excuse, and you know it. If you were really interested in me, in us, you would be making the most of the weeks you have left here for us to see each other'

'I just I have a lot on my mind and to be honest I don't have the luxury of being able to make you my main priority'

'Okay, so there it is. There is the truth, I am not a priority to you at all. The fact is that you cant be bothered to make any time to see me which shows what you really think.'
'That's not fair, as usual with you everything is black and white, and everyone needs to fit around what you want. I can't do that, I can't give you that, I have to move away, I have to think about myself, what I am going to do and where I am going'
He started walking around the room like a caged tiger, trying his best to not lose his temper.
'Stop making excuses, we could make it work if we wanted. The fact is if you really did think about me at all and took what we may have together seriously, you wouldn't be going, you would stay here and move into my place'
'Why do you keep on about that David? It is not happening, we have talked and talked about it. What if it didn't work out, what would happen then, I don't want to have to rely on you, I want to try and for once in my life, be independent, be secure, knowing that where I live is my own and no-one can just dispose of me. Why do you keep pushing me, I cannot offer you everything you want'
They stared at each other silently
David sighed 'Well, don't worry, I'm not going to push you anymore, this is it now. I just wanted to talk to you today to let you know that I will happily look after Muffin and your belongings for as long as you need me to, but I can't stand this runaround anymore, let's just agree to call it a day shall we?'
Jen fought back the tears 'If that's what you want. I don't know what else to say, you are not making this any easier for me, as usual it is all about what you want. If anything, it is you who is pushing me away'
'Ha, of course I am. You know I thought I saw something in you, but I can now see there is nothing. Maybe it is what you have been through in your past or maybe it is just the way you are, the fact is you are just cold, even if you find

what you are chasing after, it won't melt that frozen heart, you will never be happy with anyone'

He walked towards the door 'I will come and collect Muffin and your belongings after Christmas, let me know which day is best.'

He left the study and the house. She wanted to run after him, to explain what was wrong, but she would not know where to start, how to even begin, she couldn't rationalise it to herself.

Jen did not know how she got through the rest of the afternoon. His words cut into her like a knife. Eventually she asked Caroline if she may go home as she had an awful headache.

She went straight to her bedroom, stripped off her clothes, got into her bed and pulled the duvet around herself tightly, Muffin beside her.

She was still in bed in the same position when there was a knock at the door. It was already dark. Could it be David? She jumped up, turned the lights on, pulled on her dressing gown and ran down to open the door. It was Ted.

'Are you okay?' he asked

'Yes, I'm fine, just tired'

'Caroline said you had to leave, how is your headache now?'

'It's better thanks'

'Was David anything to do with it? I saw him storming out of the house'

'Yep, I guess he was, it's just so hard to know what to do' She started crying and Ted walked in and put his arms around her.

'He says that he wants me now but maybe next month or next year he will realise he has made a mistake and by then I may be relying on him. When he discovers I am not the special person, he thinks I am, and that I am just me, just Jennifer Merchant, no one special at all, he will not want me, or just look at me that way and.....'

"Oh Jen, of course you are special, you are so wrong'
'But you don't really know me either, you just see the best
side of me, like he does, you don't know all the bad bits or
the sad bits of me'
'Maybe I know you better than you think'
She pulled away from him wiping her eyes on her sleeve.
'Anyway, it doesn't matter now, it's over and probably for
the best in the long run, don't worry I am fine, I must just
be tired'
'Listen, let's talk about all of this tomorrow, get some rest
and I had better get back over to Caroline, she is rather
upset at the moment, and we still have lots yet to discuss'
'Oh dear, is everything okay?'
'Yep, she is a woman used to getting all her own way, but it
is not just down to her to make all the decisions now.
Anyway, forget about that, it will be sorted out, do you
remember when I said I would take you to Oxford with me
someday?'
'Yes of course I do'
'Well, I am going tomorrow, will you come with me?'
'That would have been lovely, but I can't, I am working'
'Don't worry about that, I have already spoken to Caroline
and told her you will not be coming in'
'Oh really, was she okay with that?'
'Yes, she was fine, but you will need to pack an overnight
bag'
 'Oh okay, then I will need find someone to look after
Muffin'
'Would David look after him?'
'Er no, I wouldn't want to ask him, but I could call Helen,
she is always happy to have him for the odd day'
'I have booked us into an Airbnb for the night, but we
won't be back too late. I will call for you after breakfast
okay, I had better get back to Caroline now, get back in the
ring for round two. Night sweetheart, see you in the
morning, get some rest'

CHAPTER 20

Jen awoke early the next morning and packed an overnight bag and some smarter black jeans and a top in case they were eating out, plus some dog food and his bed for Muffin.

Ted arrived and they put Muffin in the back of his hired hatchback and dropped him off at Upper Leys Farm on the way.

'Thanks so much for this, actually it is just what I needed' said Jen 'It feels so great to get away from everything, and spend some time with you of course, I have hardly seen you since you came back'

'No, I know, I am sorry, I have just been so tied up with lawyers and meetings and paperwork, but I think everything is sorted out now'

'So, have you finished your book?'

'Nearly, just needs editing and an epilogue'

'That's great news, but does that mean you won't need to come back? What about Patrick? How is he by the way?'

'Oh, he is fine, busy as always, but it was lovely to meet up again last weekend. To be honest though, I don't know what's going to happen when the book is finished, I don't know how often I will need to come back to England after that, so who knows if what we have together will last'

'You will just have to set your next book in England too. Maybe even in London, then you could see lots of him. Or hopefully it will be a best seller and you can spend some time touring the country publicising it and signing your book'

'Ha, yes, that would be amazing'

'You don't know, maybe it will be so successful that you will be able to buy yourself a swanky penthouse apartment in London'

'Let's not get too carried away, but thanks for your belief in me'

It felt a relief to be leaving the village. Leaving her worries, her small sad world behind for a few days. She had not been out of the area since her visit to Laura with the birth certificate in the summer. Maybe that was what part of the problem, she had got too dependent on everyone and everything, it will be good for her to spread her wings and learn to fly again. She hoped.

She was in two minds whether to take the three hour drive to see the room she was hoping to rent on Saturday. Of course, she knew it was sensible to view it and spend some time exploring the area and the town. Although the thought of driving all that way and having to face the reality of the situation, seemed somehow worse than just making a blind leap of faith once she had no choice but to go.

Or maybe it was more sensible to stay in a cheap bed and breakfast or hotel for a few nights at first and have a proper look around, if that room had gone by then, that was fate, there were plenty more rooms to rent in the area. She had worked out that if she was careful, she would have enough savings to pay for rent and food for over six months, if the worst-case scenario happened and she could not find a job straight away. That was of course unless there were any unaccounted-for bills, such as anything going wrong with her car, but she was sure she would get some work, she was prepared to do anything.

After a couple of hours, they reached the city and Ted found their home for the night and parked in the allotted space. They didn't have access to the apartment until after 4pm but they had plenty to see and explore before then. They walked the short distance to the city centre and stopped for coffee and cake before climbing the Carfax Tower. The steps were steep and narrow but the view from the top was worth it, even on dull day in December.

'This tower is all that remains of the twelfth century St. Martin's Church' informed Ted 'No other building in central Oxford is allowed to be built any higher, so it is a great place to start our tour'

'Wow I love it. This view must have looked pretty much the same for hundreds and hundreds of years.'

'Thats right, it looks even more incredible to a Canadian, we celebrate when one of our buildings has been standing for 150 years'

'Is that why you based your book here? You have never really spoken about it, apart from saying that it is a historical novel'

'Kind of. Do you know that my father and his brother studied here in Oxford? They both went to Trinity College, but there was a five year age difference so they were not actually here at the same time'

'How amazing, imagine being able to study here at Oxford, that would be a dream. A bit different to the third rate colleges I am hoping will accept me next year'

'Yes, my father often spoke about his time here, he loved it'

They climbed back down the steps and walked on towards the Ashmolean Museum.

'This is the oldest museum in the United Kingdom' explained Ted 'In fact it is one of the oldest in the world'

Jen could have spent hours walking around, but Ted warned her that there was still so much to see and they only had the one day, so they absorbed as much as they could and then walked on to the college grounds past

Balliol, stopping for a while at Trinity to imagine the young
Pendlehurst brothers right here, all those years ago.
'I bet if they were stood here today everything would look
exactly the same' said Jen looking around the grounds.
'Yes, on the outside at least'
They carried on along Broad Street, New College Lane and
Queens Lane, pausing to admire The Sheldonian Theatre,
The Bridge of Sighs, The Bodleian Library and the
stunning Radcliffe Camera, as well as the various colleges.
Eventually they stopped for a late lunch at what Ted
informed her was believed to be the oldest coffee house in
Europe.
'There is still so much to see' said Ted 'Are you happy to
keep exploring or have you had enough? Have I bored you
yet?'
'Not at all, do we ever need to stop? If you're writing
career was ever to bomb, I am sure you could always get a
job as a tour guide'
'Ha, I would love to do that. I am so glad you are enjoining
the day. Come on then finish your coffee and let's keep
going'
They continued to The Oxford Botanic Gardens, which
even in winter were stunning.
'Don't tell me, let me guess, this is the oldest botanical
garden in the world' joked Jen
'No, just the oldest in the United Kingdom, it was started
in the 1600s'
'I wonder if David has ever visited here. He would love it'
'So what happened? You seemed to be getting on well a
few weeks ago and now it's over again?'
'To be honest I don't know. When I was with him, I felt
anxious and claustrophobic and when I was not with him I
felt anxious and fearful. When we were together, I wanted
to run away, but when I did run away it felt like I was
heading for a cliff and I needed him to be at the bottom to
catch me. It's complicated'

'You are complicated. You are scared, you don't know how to trust a man, and you are too fearful to even want to try'

'But I should be scared, I could have been hurt so badly. Then I will be even worse off than I am now. I can control things now, well just about. I can go away and work hard and plan for something better, I can rely on myself and be strong. If David let me down, I dont think I would have the strength to go through that at the moment. It is just not the right time to be vulnerable. Do you understand what I mean?

I never expected this, I honestly never though anyone would really want me. I guess I just thought my life would be lived through Laura somehow, that I would always just be around when she needed me, and her happiness was my happiness'

'But you know that is not fair on Laura right?' said Ted 'You just can't plan the future avoiding everything, you just have to hope for the best sometimes, otherwise if you over analyse everything you will end up not bothering to do anything at all.

Wouldn't you at least like to know that you tried. What is going to happen if you just walk away from him now, you may regret not having given it your best shot. Laura has her own life, she could stay in Australia for goodness sake, and you will be here on your own'

'I don't know' replied Jen 'Believe me it all goes round and round in my head, but all I do know is that I can only really think about January at the moment. I need to deal with that first. I have to find somewhere to live, somewhere to work, make some sort of life for myself again. Then maybe I will feel secure enough to think about a relationship'

They continued their tour walking in a large loop until they were back on St Giles going towards their accommodation. It was dark now and the Christmas lights and cold air made everywhere even more magical.

'Okay its gone 6 o'clock I think we deserve a drink' said Ted stopping outside The Lamb and Flag.

They ordered real ale and sat in a quiet corner near the fire, enjoying being out of the cold.

'Alright tell me where we are, what's the story?' asked Jen

'Well, this pub has been here since the 1500s, Thomas Hardy, Tolkien and C.S. Lewis are all known to have been regulars here, so this is where I need to set up my time machine. By the way do you want to go out and eat tonight, or shall we just get a takeaway, your choice'

'Ooh I would prefer a takeaway if that's okay with you, let's stay in and be cosy'

They finished their drinks and walked the short distance to their apartment. It was lovely, characterful, warm and comfortable.

'Why don't you have a nice bath and warm up, and I will go and pick up some wine and food' suggested Ted.

They decided on a Thai and Jen relaxed in the big bath while Ted was gone, then found placemats, cutlery and wine glasses and laid the table. While she was waiting, she messaged Laura telling her about the fabulous day she had enjoyed with Ted and how interesting and beautiful Oxford was. Should she text David and ask him if he had ever visited the botanical gardens in Oxford? Ted walked in and idea was lost.

He poured them large glasses of wine while Jen organised the takeaway dishes on the table. When they had finished, they cleared everything away and lay out together on the sofa, it felt so natural to be in his company, so relaxed.

'I have another story about Oxford to tell you' said Ted, sipping his wine 'When Uncle Charles was studying here in the 1950s he met a young waitress called Sheila, as a matter of fact at the time they met she was working at the coffee house where we had lunch today'

'Really? It's funny, I can't imagine Mr Pendlehurst as a hot blooded young man'

'Well I guess he must have been at some time because they dated for a few months and then at the beginning of the summer she discovered that she was pregnant with his baby'

'Oh no, really? What happened?'

'Well, as you can imagine, in those days the whole situation would have been deemed as shameful anyway, whatever the circumstances. Added to that was the fact that Sheila was a young working class waitress and the Pendlehursts a rather pompous upper middle class family definitely made the whole sad scenario even worse. Uncle Charles was the eldest son, a young man with a bright future ahead of him, they certainly would not have wanted any scandal.

It was simply not the done thing. Looking back after all these years who knows what his intentions were and if he loved Sheila and wanted to be with her. I guess we cannot judge him, as we obviously don't know. What we do know though is that eventually he had to confess all to my grandparents, and they stepped in and dealt with this embarrassing situation. Whether Charles was glad to have this problem dealt with on his behalf, or was terribly upset to lose the love of his life, again we will never know, but Charles was whisked off to Italy for the summer and when he returned he completed his last year at Cambridge'

'And the poor girl?'

'My grandparents' lawyer was consulted, and arrangements were made apparently. They paid her off, after making her sign a disclaimer of course'

'How awful, times were just so different then, thank goodness that type of stigma doesn't exist anymore. I guess though that must mean that you have a cousin out there somewhere if Sheila had the baby and they are still alive. Do you know what happened to them?'

'Well, it's a rather sad story I'm afraid. Sheila seems to have quickly been married off to a drinking buddy of her fathers. He was quite a bit older than her and by all accounts a bit of a brute, very controlling, particularly when it came to the money she had been given by my grandparents, which seems to have gone mostly on his drinking and the betting shop'

'So, is this it?' asked Jen excitedly 'Is this your book, the story you have been researching'

'Yes, it is'

'How long have you known about this, did your family discuss it?'

'No, you're kidding, it was never discussed. Actually, I overheard a snippet of conversation between my father and Uncle Charles when we were visiting Millstone that summer. They were in Uncle Charles's study, it was a warm day and the windows were open, I was reading on a bench on the patio not far away.

I wasn't taking any notice of their conversation, not listening to them at all, but then there was something in my father's voice that made me sit up and listen. I just caught the tail end of what they were talking about before the window was closed, but I had heard enough'

'So did you never ask him about it'

'No, there is no way I could have felt comfortable doing that'

'Do you think Mrs Pendlehurst knew?'

'No, she didn't know anything about it at all'

'I guess the journalist in you obviously just needed to know more'

'Yes, it was always at the back of mind, always a bit of a mystery that I wanted to solve. My childhood was very traditional, very English, even though we were living in Toronto. Mum and dad were very conservative, very old school, I wouldn't even know how to start asking about such a scandal in the family. Remember I had the task of telling them I was gay for goodness sake, I couldn't throw anything else at them'

'When did you tell them that?'

'I was twenty and was home from college for Christmas, I had met my first love and, as you do, thought we would be together forever. I decided I wanted to be with him and had to be a man and stand up for who I truly was.

I remember waiting to choose the right moment, dad was at work and my mother was in the kitchen baking mince pies when I just told her straight out that I was in love with a man and that I hoped she would accept me for who I was'

'What did she say?'

'She said that she had always presumed that I was a homosexual but had never wanted to breach the subject in case it upset me. Then she asked me if I would allow her to tell my father after the Christmas break.

Which of course I was relieved for her to do. He never talked about it to me, never mentioned anything about it at all, he just carried on as if everything were normal, sometimes I wondered if mum had ever even told him. Mum was fine, she met various partners over the years, and it was all very natural, I guess she just wanted what every mum wants for their kids, for them to be happy'

'Actually, you are wrong, not all mums are concerned about that' said Jen 'You are lucky to have had such lovely parents. I remember them well from when you all stayed that summer, they were both very sweet.'

'Yes, you are right they were, I still really miss them'

'So when did you start researching this? How long did it take you to find out about poor Sheila?'

'I didn't start until they had both died. To be honest I didn't really start until I met Patrick in Vancouver and needed an excuse to come over. Shallow I know'

'Maybe it was just fate, it was the right time' said Jen 'So did you track them down? Did you get to meet Sheila or her child'

'No, sadly I didn't meet either of them, Sheila died tweny years ago, and her daughter more than ten years ago'

'Poor Shelia, what a life, I am sure she didn't deserve any of that'

'Yes, it was very tragic by all accounts, Sheila lived a wretched life after Uncle Charles abandoned her. Her husband was violent and abusive, and it sounds as if she didn't have the strength or maybe the confidence to do anything about it. She just put up with her lot, as many women sadly do.

They left Oxford and moved to Birmingham shortly after they married, probably so nobody would know that the baby was not his, and I guess she didn't have any family or friends around to support her. She worked all her life as a cleaner in a factory and died of lung cancer when she was in her 50s'

'Oh my god, just imagine how different her life would have been if Charles had grown some balls and stood by her. She could have lived at Millstone with her child and maybe future children. Or of course, the other alternative would have been if they had never got together in the first place, or she had not fallen pregnant'

'Yep, sometimes life is just sliding doors'

'I know it is different when you have your own children, but somehow I can't imagine them as parents, neither of them seemed that way inclined, they certainly never took much notice of Laura when she was little, and she would have melted anyone's heart, she was so gorgeous'

'Well, I don't know about that. Apparently, they had tried for many years for a family, but they were not 'blessed' as my mother used to say'

'Oh really, I didn't know that. I am so sorry, I didn't mean to sound so mean to them, it just goes to show you don't know what happens in people's lives. Maybe I misread them all those years. Maybe having Laura as part of their lives made them sad, showed them what they had missed. That's so awful, I should have been more understanding, I never even thought it could be that'

'You were not to know'

'So, what is the story of Sheila's daughter, the cousin, what happened to her?'

'She had a very troubled childhood, went off the rails as they say. She got pregnant at 17. There are some rumours that the baby's father may have even been the stepfather, but I don't know for certain. She was running around with a bad crowd apparently, so the child's father may well have been one of the local boys. When the parents found out she was pregnant the stepfather threw her out and she moved away from the area and into a squat where she met some guy she hooked up with for a couple of years, a local drug dealer'

'Oh, this gets worse and worse. I am not sure I really want to know, but okay, what happened then?'

Ted reached over and took her hand 'Christine gave birth to her child on September 10th. A baby girl whom she named Jennifer'

They sat in silence, Jen searching Teds eyes for some kind of punchline. Was he joking with her? Had she heard him correctly?

'Jen' Ted said eventually 'Do you understand what I am telling you?'

'I don't know. No. Yes. You are saying that Sheila's daughter was my mother'

'Yes'

'And she is dead?'

'Yes. I am afraid she died of an overdose'

'Of course she did' said Jen bitterly

'So what you are saying is. What you are saying is. You are saying that Charles Pendlehurst is, was, my grandfather'

'Yes'

'So he caused all that pain, all that carnage, ruined all of our lives and he didn't even know what he had done' she spat out, her eyes filling with tears.

'No Jen' Ted said, putting his arms around her and pulling her closer 'He did know. How do you think you ended up at Millstone?'

'What? What do you mean how did I end up there? I got a job, thats ....'

'And who got you the job?'

'That lovely man from the charity, my support worker Harry, he helped me to find the job when I left with Laura'

'Harry was working for Uncle Charles. The charity was a facade. Uncle Charles paid him to keep an eye on you. To keep him updated with reports of your welfare, which was fine while you were at college and in your flat. The idea was to help you finish college, to pay for your accommodation, and make sure you had enough money, without it all looking suspicious.

When you had finished college, they would support you through university or help you to get a suitable job.

Apparently you had told Harry that you were keen to travel, which would have been a perfect scenario for Uncle Charles, he would have been able to support you, but you would have been out of the way.

When Laura was born, everything changed when you took her away. Although apparently, they both agreed that it was for the best, there could have been repercussions, from your mother or the authorities.

They paid Christine some money, to be honest it did not take much negotiating, and then decided that the best thing for you and Laura would be for you to live and work at the cottage. That way if there was any problem from social services or such like, you were both under the care of your grandfather'

'But thats a lie, apart from somewhere to live and work, he didn't care for us at all, he hardly noticed us, he rarely even spoke more than two words'

'Jen, I am not defending him, but it honestly must have been difficult for him to have both of you practically living under his roof. He had to protect Aunt Rosemary, there could be no suspicion that you were anything more than hired help. He had kept it a secret all those years, he could not hurt or betray her, he had to put her first. Remember that they could not have children of their own, suddenly taking in two unknown grandchildren of your husbands would have been devastating for her.

Apparently Charles and Rosemary first met the year that Christine was born, I don't know the exact date, and they did not get engaged until two years later, so Christine was obviously a secret he had kept from Rosemary for a very long time'

'Why didn't he help Sheila, or my mother, or me when I really needed him, when I was little?'

'For years he didn't know anything about you. I guess he just hoped in the back of his mind that Sheila went on to live a happy life and he got on with his, he built a very successful career and business, married and built a home together with his wife.

Then about twenty-five years ago he received a letter from Sheila, she knew that she was dying and asked him to help you. She had kept in contact with your mother with occasional telephone calls and she sent her money when she could, but Christine was very bitter and blamed her mother for a lot of her problems.

I understand that she visited you once or twice when you were very young but that was all, Christine punished her by keeping her away from you, I think. We must though give your mum some credit and presume that she may have also been keeping you away from Sheila because of her stepfather'

'Sheila had promised to take their secret to her grave but Uncle Charles and told him about you and your situation and begged him to help you.

Unfortunately, I think he may have sat on that letter for a while, but eventually after Sheila's death he organised for a private investigator to find you. By that time you were due to leave the care home where you had been living. Harry then stepped in as your care worker and organised for you to have a flat and encourage you to pursue your education. He contacted you occasionally I understand, but he was actually also watching you from afar while you were at college'

'That sounds crazy. I honestly never knew, I just thought he was a lovely, kind man. What about my mum, did he not try to help his own daughter?'

'I don't know for sure. I do know that Christine did spend some time in a private clinic around this time, but she didn't stay there for very long, she left after three weeks, but I know that he paid for that. I think though that Christine was a lost cause I am sad to say. Not to mention the fact that she was a loose cannon, I don't think he would have risked her getting too close'

'It's all so sad, it's tragic, so many lives ruined. I still don't understand how he could be so remote with us at Millstone, he honestly hardly looked at us. We were his grandchildren for goodness sake'

'I see how he let your mother and your grandmother down big time. But just imagine if after 40 years of marriage, you had to admit a secret illegitimate child and brought your grandchildren to live in your house. It must have been dangerous for him to have embedded you both into their lives and in the cottage in the first place. I know he paid the Attleys a large sum of money to move on quickly and quietly.'

'Really? How did you find all this information?'

'When we were staying at Millstone that last time, Uncle Charles must have given my father a folder with some information and various documents, maybe he wanted to be sure that someone would know what happened when he died. The folder had been left with my fathers' will and his other personal papers with his lawyer and was then passed on to me when he died five years ago.

I didn't really go through all of his papers thoroughly until last year, when I eventually read it.

When I came here I traced old family and friends of Sheila and Christine, and of course some of the information is for public viewing, birth certificates and various records. My greatest find though was Harry, who is the only person still alive who actually knows the whole story. He was incredibly pleased to hear news about you and Laura, he told me that you were one of the bravest young women he had ever met, and often wondered how you both were'

'Ah, Harry, did he really say that?'

'Yes, and its true. Not many teenagers would have sacrificed so much'

Ted pulled her closer and they sat in silence.

'Thank you, Ted. I know I am upset and there is so much to take in, but I would always prefer to know the truth. Thank you for researching your book and telling me all that. It feels raw right now but it is good to know I have some roots, some background, like other people have'

'Thats okay Cuz' said Ted smiling.

'Ha, oh yes thats the best thing to come out of all this mess we have you, we have a cousin, you can't get away from me now' saYou have single handedly doubled the size of our family. Ha, just imagine if I had found out that Caroline was my cousin, don't think I would have been so thrilled at that'

'Ah I am glad you are pleased it is me, and I have you' said Ted hugging her tightly 'And don't worry I intend sticking around'

'Thats great, I am so pleased. Wherever I end up we must stay in contact because we are not just friends now, we are family'

'Jen, you are not going anywhere. Not now. That is one of the reasons I wanted us to stay away overnight. I spoke to Caroline yesterday and gave her a copy of Uncle Charles's will, which could only be released when Aunt Rosemary had died. She has agreed to pack up the last of their belongings and be out by the morning. Jen, Millstone House is yours and Laura's'

Jen pulled away from him, searching his face for the second time that evening. Had she misunderstood what he had just said?

'Aunt Rosemary's own money, some shares and all of her personal possessions were left to Dorothea and Caroline. But everything else, the house, the cottage, the remainder of the shares, were all left to Uncle Charles grandchildren, left to you and Laura'

'Oh my god! Oh my god! Really?'

'Yes really. It's all yours'

'No! Are you kidding me? I dont know what to say. What about Caroline, what did she say?'

'It was a bit awkward, to say the least. Aunt Rosemary had always led them to believe that everything would be shared between us when she died, I am guessing that is what she had always presumed. I have no doubt that Uncle Charles had organised everything and was happy just to let her believe that so that no questions were ever asked.

That is one of the comments I had overheard when my father and Uncle Charles were in the study and I was in the garden, Uncle Charles had said to my father that he wanted him to know that he would not be a beneficiary of his will and that he had closer dependents who would inherit his estate, when he and Rosemary died. I had tried to let Caroline down gently by warning her that the will may hold a few surprises, but I thought it was best to get the funeral over before I actually showed her a copy last night'

'Oh, my goodness Ted, I must talk to Laura. What time is it?'

They video called Laura.

'Lolly, who is this?' asked Jen turning the camera to face Ted

'It's Ted'

'Exactly, and who is Ted?'

'Have you been drinking mum? You look a bit hysterical?'

'I have been drinking and I am feeling a little hysterical, but that is not the point. This gorgeous man sat here beside me isn't just Mr Edward Pendlehurst, he is in fact our cousin Mr Edward Pendlehurst'

'Ted, what have you been giving my mother to drink?'
laughed Laura

'Actually cousin Laura she is telling you the truth'

They sat closely together on the sofa so they could tell
Laura the whole story, their story, answering her questions
as best they could.

'Does this mean we are going to be famous when your
book comes out?' asked Laura

'Oh no' said Jen 'I hadn't even thought about that, I would
hate that'

'No don't worry, it's a fictional novel, I have changed all
the names and places'

'Thank goodness for that' said Jen

'I still can't believe it, I keep thinking you are both going to
start laughing any minute and say it is all a joke. Mum, do
you want me to come home? I know this is amazing news
but it's a lot to take in, or shall I come back for Christmas?
I keep worrying about you being on your own'

'No Laura, you have so many plans, please don't worry
about me, I will be fine. In fact, I may now be able to come
and see you in the New Year as we had planned'

'But I hate you to be on your own for Christmas, whether
you are in the cottage or at Millstone it's all the same, you
will still be on your own'

'She won't be' said Ted 'I am going to stay until the New
Year. If that's okay with everyone?'

'Yes!' they both shouted.

Jen felt exhausted when they eventually went to bed. She
was drained from the crying and turmoil of emotions, and
dizzy from the huge sense of relief. A mountain had been
lifted from her shoulders, she did not have to leave. For
the first time they were secure, they had a real home, as
unbelievable as that still sounded.

But she could not sleep. Her mind was going over and over
everything, her grandmother Sheila, her grandfather
Charles, her mother, Harry, Laura, Mrs Pendlehurst, Ted,
they were all connected, and she had never known.

She tried desperately to remember all of the times she had interacted in any way with Mr Pendlehurst, her grandfather. He was normally at work when she was at Millstone or in his study so she saw very little of him and to be honest she was a little afraid of him, he had seemed rather aloof on the occasions their paths did cross.

She did have one particular memory of him though. It was summer and she and Laura were in the walled garden, there was a purple buddleia bush covered with butterflies and she was showing them to Laura, lifting her up so that she could see them at the top.

She remembered glancing towards the house and there was Mr Pendlehurst at his bedroom window watching them, she remembered wondering if he may be cross, if they were maybe making too much noise, but he just stood there watching and when he noticed her looking he had waved at them, she had turned Laura around to show her, and they had both waved back.

That memory made her weep again, this time for Mr Pendlehurst, her grandfather, who in the end was also a victim of circumstance. His grandchildren were there, within his grasp and yet any contact he may have wanted with them had to be suppressed.

She eventually fell asleep in the early hours of the morning but was awoken by a strange and vivid dream, she and Laura were both young children and asleep in twin beds in one of the bedrooms at Millstone. The bedroom was beautifully decorated as a nursery and Charles Pendlehurst was standing in the doorway, watching them sleep.

In the morning Jen asked if they may have breakfast at the coffee shop where Sheila had worked, before they left Oxford. They walked through the cold wet streets already busy with Christmas shoppers. When they arrived Jen stood for a moment trying to imagine a dapper young man walking up this street and opening this door and seeing a young woman. Was it instant attraction, she wondered.

They sat down and ordered a pot of tea while they looked at the menu. There had obviously been some changes to the building, but it was still easy to imagine the ghosts of her grandparents moving about the room.

CHAPTER 21

They arrived back at Millstone House at lunchtime after collecting Muffin from Upper Leys Farm. It was not the right time to discuss all that she had discovered the night before with Helen, she was still struggling to process it herself. She needed time to adjust first, she still could not believe it was true. Maybe Ted had made a genuine mistake, a misunderstanding and when they walked in Caroline would be there laughing at them, explaining to Ted that the lawyer had misread the will and it would be best if Jen packed her stuff and left the cottage that day. Caroline's car had gone, but she was still nervous as they opened the door and walked through into the kitchen, Muffin waited at the door.

'Come on Muffin, come in, it's your home too' said Ted
For a moment Jen was going to protest, Muffin had never been allowed in the house, they may get into trouble. He bounded in, sniffing the kitchen floor and walking around the table. Ted opened the door into the hallway and he ran through into the drawing room, jumping up on a sofa and making himself at home.

'Ooh, I wonder what Aunt Rosemary would have said about that?' said Ted laughing

195

'Not to mention Caroline' said Jen 'This is weird. It just doesn't seem real, I feel like an intruder and that someone is going to come and tell us off and throw me out'

'It's going to take some time. You know you could always sell the house if you are not happy here, it's for you to decide'

'I will never sell this house Ted, I love this house, I have always loved this house. I have spent nearly twenty years cleaning it and caring for it, when I was working I often had little daydreams going through my head where I pretended that it was mine and fantasized what I would do with it'

'Well now you can fulfil all of those fantasies, it is yours, I can't think of anyone more deserving of it'

They walked around the rest of the house slowly as if for the first time. Jen walked through each room, looking out of the windows and touching the furniture, she could not hold back her tears.

'Whatever is the matter' said Ted hugging her

'I can't believe this, not any of it. I am so happy, we have a home, a real home of our own, that nobody can take away from us. You know Ted I would have been ecstatic to have owned a two bedroomed flat one day or at the most a little cottage like mine next door. That was always my dream, from when I was a child. Now I have this, its like all too much to take in. Would it be strange if I stayed at the cottage for a while? Just until I get my head around everything'

'No of course not, I will stay there with you'

'Yes, I would like that'

They went back to the cottage cooked pasta and talked late into the night.

The next morning Jen got up early and walked over to Millstone before Ted was awake, she walked around each room again, but this time making plans in her head.

When she arrived back at the cottage Ted was drinking coffee.

'Morning' said Jen

'Wow you look bright and breezy today'

'I am. I had to get up, I woke up really early and my mind just kept going over and over plans I have for the house, I felt so excited I had to go back over to see if it was still real'

'That's great, okay what are they?'

'Do you have some time today? Do yo fancy coming shopping?'

'Hell yes, I love the sound of that'

They had breakfast and then drove into Boughton, firstly stopping at a very exclusive garden centre on the outskirts of the town.

'Every Christmas I used to think that if Millstone was mine I would have a huge tree in the entrance lobby, and another one in the drawing room, that is what we are going to sort out first'

Jen ordered a nine foot Norway Spruce for the lobby and a six foot one for the drawing room, for delivery the following day. They also bought Christmas lights, delicate glass baubles, a huge wreath for the front door and lots of candles.

The next stop was a bed shop to choose a new bed for the master bedroom and one for Teds room, the beds were rather old at Millstone anyway and this was another dream on Jens fantasy list, a super king sized bed, with a luxury mattress.

Her own bed was small and Mrs Pendlehurst's had not been much bigger, it had always looked lost in such a big bedroom. Ted protested that he did not need one.

'Listen those beds have got to be well over twenty years old, the least I can do for all you have done for me is buy you a new bed, Laura will have that bedroom when she is at home anyway so I will want to get a new one eventually.

They then moved on to the department store and purchased new bedding and towels. Then finally stopped off at the hardware shop where they selected paint, brushes, paint trays and sandpaper.

The next day they started decorating Mrs Pendlehursts bedroom. All her personal belongings had been removed after she had died and Caroline had taken the smaller pieces of furniture, just leaving a wardrobe and chest of drawers. It was a beautiful room, with a large floor length window overlooking the walled garden and a wrought iron fireplace. It was as big as both of the bedrooms in the cottage put together.

In the afternoon the Christmas trees arrived, and the delivery men installed them. The huge one in the lobby was magnificent, filling the house with the scent of pine. They left the painting to finish the next day and Ted climbed the ladder to arrange the lights around the tree and fitted the wreath to the front door. Jen was so pleased she had kept the old decorations from the loft and enjoyed every moment of decorating the tree in the drawing room with them.

She stood back and looked at it in all its glory hanging with the handmade decorations and mementoes that meant so much to her. She took a photograph of the moment in her mind for her soul and realised it had been months since it had even crossed her mind to capture a happy moment in her life. Just two weeks ago she had packed the decorations up never knowing when they would be used again. They were both exhausted when they finally went back to the cottage to sleep.

They spent the rest of the week decorating and organising Millstone and on the Friday the new beds were delivered, they dressed them with the new bedding and moved Jens clothes over to her new bedroom. Late that night she lay in her huge new bed, looking around her bedroom and didn't think she had ever been happier, she certainly couldn't remember a time when she had, for the first time in many months she felt totally at peace.

The last part of her plan was scheduled for the following Sunday. She had telephoned Helen and Fliss and invited them and their partners to come over to the cottage for drinks. She had managed to avoid them all week, telling them that she was busy with Ted, which certainly was not a lie. She had never been able to invite all of them before as there was simply not enough room, in fact her little kitchen table only had three chairs. To be able to accomplish the surprise and avoid any suspicion, she had suggested they all come to the cottage for drinks before going on to The Plough for lunch with her and Ted.

They all still believed that she was leaving in the New Year so had assumed this occasion was for them to say goodbye. Jen didn't tell them this was a farewell meal, but neither did she dismiss the possibility, after all, it was true, she was leaving the cottage. Ted and Jen spent the morning preparing Sunday lunch, roast beef with all the trimmings and Teds speciality cheesecake.

Jen took huge pleasure in dressing the enormous dining table, with the very best china and glasses, she lit the fires in the dining room and drawing room, and decorated the mantlepieces with lights, fir, ivy and holly from the garden. At one o'clock she was back at the cottage awaiting their arrival with mulled wine warming on the stove, leaving Ted in charge of the final arrangements of the meal. Helen and Mike had picked up Fliss and Peter, and they all managed to squeeze into the sitting room, Jen perched on the coffee table.

She felt slightly hysterical, trying her best not to start giggling, when the rest of the room where obviously feeling anxious about upsetting her. She was so excited to surprise them all and had been planning the big reveal for over a week, but they of course were subdued and being incredibly polite, obviously afraid to say anything that would be negative about their last lunch together.

She could not bear it another moment.

'Okay everyone, drink up and we will go over and collect Ted' collecting their coats from the kitchen table.

'Shall we all walk over and see if he is ready' she suggested as soon as they were all back outside.

They looked slightly bemused at why they all needed to walk around to Millstone, especially the long way around to the front door to collect Ted, but all followed Jen obediently.

Jen rang on the brass bell and Ted opened the door and as they had planned.

'Hi, everyone lovely to see you all again, come in'

He opened the door wide and guided them past the huge Christmas tree.

'Let me take your coats'

They all looked confused again but obeyed his instructions and removed their coats which he hung in the hallway cupboard while making polite small talk.

'Please follow me folks'

He opened the double doors and led them into the beautiful dining room, table decorated, fire blazing.

'Please take a seat, and I will get you a drink?'

They all sat silently, smiling politely but casting sideways looks at each other.

Ted opened white and red wine and put the bottles on the table, he then opened a bottle of champagne and served each of them a glass before sitting down opposite Jen.

'Would you all please join me in a toast' he said, raising his glass

They all silently raised their glasses

'To the new owners of Millstone House. To Jen and Laura'

There was silence.

'Okay thats enough of the sodding dramatics, what the fucks going on' said Fliss

Jen burst out laughing 'Oh Fliss, I love you so much, I knew you would be the first to break'

'Just tell me whats happening, is this a joke, have you married Ted?'

'Oh Fliss' laughed Ted 'That would be wrong in so many ways'

'No, I have not married Ted' laughed Jen 'And I am really sorry for all the theatrics but I wanted to do something special for you all, for my dear friends who have looked after me and Laura all these years, inviting us into your homes and treating us like family. I love you all so much and wanted to share with you something incredible that has happened, something I have discovered. Well, I should I say my gorgeous cousin Ted here discovered'

'Did you say cousin?' asked Helen

'Yes Helen. Okay everyone, here it is, Ted is my cousin and Charles Pendlehurst was my and Laura's grandfather' she said slowly.

They all took a while for this information to sink in.

'No, what? How could that be? asked Fliss

'Top up your glasses, I will get the starter and then we will fill you all in with the details'

They were all stunned at the news and delighted and relieved that Jen was staying in the village. They opened more bottles of champagne toasting the future, Charles Pendlehurst and Ted. This is all so perfect thought Jen, if only Laura were here to share this day with us too.

After lunch Fliss asked if Jen would show her around the house, she had always wanted to be nosy, but had never had the chance. Helen came too, and Jen proudly showed them around, telling them of her plans of gradually redecorating each room. The last room she he showed them was her bedroom and her fabulous new bed, they all lay down together giggling, the three of them side by side.

'As well as being busy decorating did you fit in a boob job too?' asked Fliss

'What do you mean?'

'Well something is different about them' laughed Fliss 'You have never been particularly blessed in that area before, is it a new bra?'

'No' laughed Jen, covering herself with her arms 'Stop looking at my boobs both of you'

'You're not pregnant, are you?' asked Helen

'Shit' said Fliss 'Shit, I thought there was something different about you, that's it, you're pregnant'

Jen sat up 'No, of course not. I can't be'

'Are you sure?' asked Fliss 'When was your last period?'

'Um, I dont really know to be honest……. they have been so erratic. I am guessing because I lost that weight, they have not really been regular for about six months. Of course, it could be my age too'

Fliss and Helen looked at each other

'Oh my god, you don't really think I could be, do you?'

'You may be' said Helen 'It was certainly he first thing I noticed in both of my pregnancies, bigger boobs. Were you using contraception?'

'Kind of, well we were being as careful as we could, but everything just happened so fast, I never really gave it a thought to be honest'

'Tomorrow morning, as soon as the shops open, go and buy a pregnancy test' said Fliss 'And as soon as you know, let us know'

'And no more alcohol for you today, just in case' suggested Helen

'Actually I haven't been drinking hardly at all, I have been feeling kind of sickly lately…..'

They both stared at her.

'Wow imagine that. A baby' said Fliss 'That would be incredible'

'How do you feel about it Jen?' asked Helen

'I dont know. I don't see how I can be, surely not, I never imagined I would ever…… do you really think I am?'

The next morning Jen was at the pharmacy door when it first opened. She never imagined in her wildest dreams that she would ever be looking at this section, in the end she bought a pack of 4 testers, to be certain of the result.

She rushed back to Millstone and into her bathroom. All night she had either been hounded by vivid dreams or had lay in the dark trying to process her feelings. Could any of this be real? When she saw the results would she be relieved or disappointed if it was negative. Would she rejoice or panic if the result was positive? She honestly could not imagine what her reaction would be.

She had not said anything to Ted the evening before as the whole situation just did not seem real until she knew for sure one way or the other anyway. Now though as she sat on the bathroom floor waiting for the result, the possible blue lines, she realised that if there was no baby, she would be devastated.

Which was ridiculous, 24 hours ago the thought had not even crossed her mind that she may one day have a child of her own, now suddenly she felt desperate for one.

Two blue lines. Two blue lines. Two blue lines. She stared at it, her heart pounding. Opening another test stick she inserted it into the small pot of urine, holding her breath, not taking her eyes from the possible result. Two blue lines. A baby. There was a baby growing inside her, a baby who would hopefully if all went well, grow up in this house, play in the garden, sit at the kitchen table, just like Laura had.

What if she had known she was pregnant two weeks ago, when she was packing up to leave. What would her choices have been then, even plan B would have been impossible. What would plan C have looked like?

When she told Ted, his eyes filled with tears, making her cry too.

'Will you be okay when I go back to Canada?'

'Yes, of course. I can't imagine Fliss or Helen giving me a moments peace, they have both messaged me a dozen times this morning, I don't know who is the more excited. Besides, you cannot keep worrying about me, you have already done more than enough, look where I am'

They spent the rest of the morning Googling information about pregnancy, fascinated by the changes that were starting to happen to her body, what she should and shouldn't eat or do and how the baby was developing inside her. Keep growing little one she whispered while stroking her tummy that night in bed.

CHAPTER 22

The day before Christmas Eve Ted left early for London to accompany Patrick to a party and then drive back with him the following day. Jen had persuaded Ted that whenever he was in England, the cottage was his. It was to be his home from home, so they had spent a day cleaning, mainly trying to rid the place of Muffins dog hair. Ted had bought a small Christmas tree and lights and stacked up the wood pile. He was so excited about his and Patrick's first Christmas together, and Jen was so pleased to be able to offer them their own cosy love nest.

They had completed the last of the Christmas shopping. Jen had already posted Laura a necklace and bracelet and forwarded her some money to buy new clothes. She had found a beautiful green cashmere jumper for Ted and bought a bottle of his favourite malt whisky for Patrick. The fridge and cupboards were bursting with far too much food for the three of them including a ridiculously huge turkey and ham.

Jen had taken Muffin for a long walk in the woods after lunch and lit the fire in the drawing room on her return. This was her first day at Millstone on her own, this was how it would be when Ted returned to Canada after

Christmas. She had imagined that she would feel lost in this big house after years in the tiny cottage, but she didn't at all, it already felt natural to be here, her home. She had just closed the curtains against sleet pounding on the window and turned on the table lamps when the doorbell rang. There stood in the pool of light from the hallway was David.

'Can I come in?'

She had tried her best not to think about him for the last couple of weeks, just shut out all feelings. Maybe it was one of her defence mechanisms, she had always been able to push memories and people to the back her mind, life was sometimes more bearable that way. She of course knew that if this baby was healthy and the pregnancy successful, she would need to talk to him, tell him.

Though not now, not yet, it still wasn't quite real, it was still too early to get too excited. But there he was, in the same place as they had first spoken all those months ago.

'Yes of course, come in'

They walked through to the drawing room.

'Can I get you anything to drink?

'No. I just wanted to talk to you'

'Okay' Jen sat down on the rug in front of the fire and hugged her legs to her chest.

David took off his coat, lay it on a side table and sat on the sofa near her. They just looked at each other for a moment, until Jen had to turn away, looking at the fire.

'From what I hear there have been some changes, you now don't need me to look after Muffin'

'No, that's right'

'Were you going bother to let me know?'

'Yes, of course, of course, we had agreed that I would contact you after Christmas. I was so grateful that you offered to help me, honestly, I couldn't have managed without your offer of having Muffin, you know that'

'I hear that you have been left this house and are planning to stay in the village?'

'Well yes. As you can imagine it was all a bit of a shock.
When did you hear about Millstone?'

'Today, when Ted called to tell me'

'Ted?'

'Yes'

'Why would Ted tell you?'

'I honestly don't know'

'I am sure he told you in the best of faith David, he
wouldn't have meant to upset you, he's not like that'

'No, I know that. From what I could understand, I think he
wanted to tell me, in a roundabout way, because he is
worried about you being on your own when he goes back
to Canada'

'He always worries about me, but I am absolutely fine he
didn't need to bother you, I am sorry he did that'

'Yes, and that's exactly what I told him. That you would be
absolutely fine. That you can look after yourself and don't
need anybody.'

'I am sorry. I am sorry he contacted you. I am sorry I never
told you I was staying in the village. I am sorry you think I
was just using you. You know I always seem to have to be
saying sorry to you for something or the other that you
don't like'

'There is absolutely nothing to be sorry for. It didn't work
out between us and that's it, end of story. He just really
pissed me off today, asking that I keep an eye on you and
make sure that you are okay. Why the hell is that down to
me? Its got nothing to do with me at all.

I don't know whether you got him to call me or he just
doesn't realise what has happened between us, I mean you
no harm I would just rather you both leave me alone, I
have moved on, it's all water under the bridge now. Please
explain that to him'

'Yes, of course, I will tell him, and no I certainly knew
nothing about him contacting you. I can only think he
doesn't understand that we are not seeing each other
anymore, I have never really spoken about it with him' she

lied. 'But I am truly sorry about Ted and everything else, I really wish we could stay friends'

'Friends. Look I am sure I will see you around now you are staying here, but I don't think thats really going to happen is it. Probably best we clear the air, realise it was never going to work and both just get on with our lives. Don't you think?'

'Sure okay, of course'

'Okay, I will be off. Don't bother to show me out'

He left shutting the sitting room door behind him, she could hear his footsteps down the tiled hallway. What had she done, what had she done. She curled herself up into a ball on the rug and sobbed uncontrollably. What had she done?

The door opened suddenly, David walked back in the room, he was picking up his coat.

Jen did not move, didn't look at him, kept her eyes closed and her face in her hands.

'You alright?'

'Don't go' she said quietly 'Please don't go'

'Jen lets not.......'

'Please' she said sniffing, wiping her eyes on her sleeves but still not looking at him 'Please don't go' she began to cry again, rocking herself gently, her arms tightly wrapped around her legs. 'I am sorry, I am really, really sorry, please, please stay'

Suddenly he was next to her. He unpeeled her arms from around her legs and lifted her chin to look at her, she kept her eyes shut tight, the tears still flowing.

'Look at me, look at me' he said softly wiping her tears with his hand.

She looked at him between deep sobs.

'I am here'

He kissed her tears gently, and then pulled her tightly into him, stroking her hair.

'I am so sorry' she said, her body still shaking, her arms clutching onto him 'I am so, so sorry, I am just so scared, just so scared, I just cant risk you leaving me, it was easier if I left you first'

'I am not going anywhere, I never was I don't want to be anywhere but here'

He lay her down on the rug and lay alongside her, holding her closely to him, stroking her hair until she stopped crying.

'Lets have a drink' he said 'Lets stop all this and be honest about what we really want. Go and wash your face and blow your snotty nose and I will put the kettle on'

Jen freshened up. When she came back into the drawing room David had made the tea and was sitting on the sofa looking at the fire.

'Come and sit here' he said

She sat down and he pulled her into his arms.

'You know I am really happy for you. Being left this house and now able to stay in the village, to have the security and independence is just wonderful. I am really happy for you, and if that makes you more comfortable and secure in having a relationship with me, all the better. But you know, I was never trying to trap you, I was just trying to help you, just solve the problem'

'I know that. It is not you, I guess I am just scared of being abandoned. I would rather be on my own and just have to deal with it, than if you had some day left me, that would have been worse'

'I love you woman' he said making her look at him 'I love you like no other and I want us to be together, if now having all this makes it easier for you, then I understand. If you want your own space and to take things slowly, we can do that now. Just don't shut me out. Tell me what you are thinking, what you are afraid of, or not happy with'

'I will, I promise'

'There is no need for any type of commitment, lets just enjoy what we have, please stop making everything so complicated, it doesn't need to be.'

'I will try not to, I don't mean to. I…..I want you in my life,

I want to be with you, I missed you'

'Good, then that's all that matters at the moment'

'Can you stay the night?' she asked

'Here we go, this is why you want me back, you have never been afraid to commit to that' he laughed.

'No, I don't mean that. Well, yes okay that is a factor in you staying. But what I mean is can you stay the evening, have some supper with me? You don't have to stay the night if you don't want to and don't think I am bribing you, but you wait until you see my fantastic new bed, its huge, you'll love it'

'What an offer. My sister and her family are arriving tomorrow morning, but Lizzy is there, so I am sure I will not be missed first thing. The deciding factor though is what you are offering to cook for me?'

'Scrambled eggs on toast?'

'Who could resist, done, I'm staying'

After supper David stoked up the fire while Jen cleared away their dishes. She walked into the drawing room to see him silhouetted against the fire light and stood there a moment watching him. Capture the moment and keep it in your heart. She felt a rush of love for him so strong that she almost started crying again. What is happening, she thought, it must be my hormones. She walked over behind him and knelt down spooning his back, her arms around his neck.

I'm so glad you are here with me'

It was unusual for her to instigate any affectionate moves, in fact, thought David, this was possibly the first time. She was always receptive to his touch, to his hugs, to his passion, but never came to him first, never reached out to him.

'There is something I need to tell you' she said quietly her arms still around his back 'You are right we must be honest with each other, and I want to tell you, but I don't know what you are going to think'

He turned around to face her. 'What?'

'I hope you wont be upset, I am not asking for anything from you'

'What, what has happened?'

She took a deep breath 'I am pregnant'

'What? Really?'

'Yes. I didn't mean….., it wasn't planned, I am not asking for anything from you'

David's eyes brimmed with tears. 'What? You are having a baby? Really, when?'

'I haven't been for a scan or anything yet but if all goes well early summer I think, that is of course if everything is okay'

He bent down and kissed her tenderly.

'I never thought I would have children' he said

'No, neither did I'

'It's our miracle baby'

'Yes, I so hope so. I didn't even know myself until a few days ago, and I wasn't even sure how I felt when I first found out but now it is the most important thing to me in the world'

David pulled her closely to him 'I can't believe it, you know when I saw you this evening I thought you looked kind of different, softer somehow, but guessed you were just eating better'

'I know that's what I thought it was'

'Have you been to see the doctor or anyone'

'I have made an appointment for after Christmas, I can't be sure of anything, especially with my age, but I just thought I wanted to enjoy this feeling over Christmas, just to hold on to this dream for a while'

'You are healthy and strong, that's got to make a difference, and we already know what a great mum you are'

'Well, let's just pray that everything is all right. I know it sounds silly but I keep thinking I have been given so much these last few weeks, I have been thrown a life line and are so blessed, I feel guilty asking for more, or expecting more'

'You have got to start believing that you deserve happiness. No one is going to come and take it away'

He left early the following morning but invited her to come over later for lunch to meet his sister and her family. Jen had been nervous driving over there, she was shy when she met new people at the best of times, and David's large family were people she wanted to like her, approve of her. But she need not have worried, Claire and her husband Martin their son Steve, and daughter Beccy and her husband Joe were just like Lizzy, very welcoming and easy going. Over lunch Claire joked that David had always been the moody one in the family and that she admired Jen for putting up with him.

'I apologise, it was our fault' laughed Claire 'We all spoiled him. Us three sisters were thrilled to have a baby brother to play with, and we let him get away with far too much, as did our lovely mum. I am afraid you will have to blame us, but we are always here to help you put him in his place, that's the least we can do.'

'I may have to keep you to that' said Jen 'He is lucky to have had you all looking after him, it must have been great growing up in a big family'

'Believe me, it wasn't like Little Women or The Waltons, it wasn't perfect, we certainly had our arguments. Melanie and Sarah especially, they are the eldest and were always squabbling about clothes or make up, but yes it was lovely most of the time, and we are all very close now and talk or see each other every week'

'Still sounds great to me'

'You are like Steve, he was an only child and his parents divorced and both remarried so he didn't have much family. He was a bit worried when we met, especially when my sisters interrogated him, but he loves it now, and there is plenty of room for more. Every summer we all rent a big house by the sea, for a week, you would love it, well I hope you would, you must come with us next year with Laura'

Before she went home Jen invited them all to Millstone on Boxing Day. She had already invited Fliss and Helen's families to join her, Ted and Patrick for afternoon drinks. They had plenty of space not to mention cupboards heaving with food and drink. It was lovely to be able to invite people and play hostess.

It was getting dark when Jen arrived home, Ted and Patrick were due back soon and she wanted everything to be cosy and festive for their arrival. She switched on all of the Christmas lights, built up the fires and lit the candles at Millstone, then went to the cottage to turn up the heating and close the curtains.

She had just sat down when she heard the car on the driveway. Ted and Patrick came in with their luggage and kissed her.

'Thank you for inviting me to your lovely home' said Patrick

'You are very welcome, it's so wonderful to have you here, sit down I will go and make us some tea, or would you prefer a drink?'

'Tea will be great and just stay out in the kitchen for a moment will you, I want to bring your present in for under the tree and I don't want you guessing what it is' added Ted

'Ooh really, we said we were just buying each other small things'

'This is small but recognisable so I don't want you peeking'

'Ha okay' Jen put on the kettle and got the mugs out on a tray with the milk and sugar.

'Can I come in now?' she called from the kitchen

'Yes, come in'

Jen walked through the hallway and into the drawing room and stopped dead. On the sofa in front of the fire was Laura.

'Lolly' she said bursting into tears.

Laura ran over to her laughing and hugged her tightly 'Surprise!'

'How did you get here? Why didn't you tell me?'

'It was all Ted's devious plan, you will have to blame him. We have been talking and I told him how much I was missing you and wanted to come home and the next thing I knew he had bought me a plane ticket and arranged to pick me up from Heathrow today. It's so lovely to be back, I have missed you so much mum, and Millstone is looking amazing, it already looks like our house, just rather bigger'
'Ted darling, thank you, thank you' Jen said, still hugging Laura.

'I told you it was going to be something small, she is no fun though, she wouldn't even let me wrap her up'
'I am so grateful to have Ted and Patrick staying, but I have missed you so much, it is not the same without you here to enjoy it with'

After supper Ted and Patrick went to the cottage and left Laura and Jen to catch up. Jen did not want to question her too much about how long she intended on staying, she knew that she would tell her in her own time. All that mattered was that she was here in their home, and they were together again.

Christmas Day was perfect, the four of them had dinner, played games, and watched old favourite Christmas editions on the television. David sent her a text and photographs of his day with his family. '*Hopefully this will be our last Christmas apart*' Later that evening when Ted and Patrick went back to the cottage, Jen and Laura sat on the sofa together next to the Christmas tree covered in their special decorations, Muffin laying in front of the fire at their feet. Everything was the same as always, even though now of course everything was so different. But what was important was the same.

On Boxing Day morning, the four of them prepared the house for their guests, they had not told anyone that Laura was back, so it was a wonderful surprise when they came, especially for Katie. As David and his family arrived the scene was complete, the house was filled with people and laughter just as it should have always been.

When everyone moved into dining room to help themselves to the food Jen glanced up into the mirror over the fireplace and saw them all in the reflection. Their friends, her family Laura and Ted, David, and his family, and herself in the frame too, she had found her place. She paused for a moment, captured that scene, and kept it in her heart forever.

Made in the USA
Monee, IL
03 May 2021